Moving his hand fro

to her hair, he wrapped his fingers in her long tresses. Luke pulled back on her head, exposing her throat.

He licked her neck. Sucked on her earlobe. When she let out a mew of delight, he returned his lips to hers. Slipping his tongue inside her mouth, Luke explored, tasted and conquered.

"Luke," Bridgette said into his mouth, their breaths becoming one. "Oh, Luke."

He pressed her into the window, his hand traveling from her hair to her stomach. He worked his fingers under the hem of her shirt, just to see if she felt as soft as he imagined.

She was.

His fingers traveled farther up her stomach, and the tips of his fingers grazed the lace of her bra. Luke pressed against the fly of his jeans. He wanted Bridgette. And it wasn't just tonight. He'd always wanted her. Hers was the face that came to him in dreams and fantasies alike.

And then the window exploded.

Dear Reader,

I have a secret! I am beyond thrilled to be a part of The Coltons of Kansas. This series is full of twists, turns, romance, passion—and of course, secrets. Besides the thrilling stories, the authors who are telling these tales are fabulous.

If you've ever read any of my previous Dear Reader letters, you might remember that the dream of being a Harlequin author goes back to my early teens. It all started with my grandmother, a woman who was both loving and glamorous, and a voracious reader of Harlequin novels.

One summer afternoon, she finished a medical romance and handed it to me, while saying, "Now, if I could find a man like *that*, I'd give up being a widow!" I read that book in a day and as I closed the cover, I had a single thought: when I grow up, I want to write romance novels.

With *Colton's Secret History*, I'm releasing my seventh book with Harlequin—something my adolescent self would have never thought possible. More even than the book is the company I get to keep with this series. Wow, just wow!

Dear Reader, I hope you enjoy reading this book as much as I enjoyed writing *Colton's Secret History*. And if you do love this book—and the series—don't keep it a secret. Pass it on to someone you love. They'll love back you for sharing!

All the best,

Jennifer D. Bokal

COLTON'S SECRET HISTORY

Jennifer D. Bokal

Special thanks and acknowledgment are given to Jennifer D. Bokal for her contribution to the The Coltons of Kansas miniseries.

Recycling programs for this product may not exist in your area.

ISBN-13: 978-1-335-62669-1

Colton's Secret History

This edition published by arrangement with Harlequin Books S.A.

For questions and comments about the quality of this book, please contact us at CustomerService@Harlequin.com.

Harlequin Enterprises ULC
22 Adelaide St. West, 40th Floor
Toronto, Ontario M5H 4E3, Canada
www.Harlequin.com

Printed in U.S.A.

Jennifer D. Bokal is the author of the bestselling ancient-world historical romance *The Gladiator's Mistress* and the second book in the Champions of Rome series, *The Gladiator's Temptation*. Happily married to her own alpha male for twenty years, she enjoys writing stories that explore the wonders of love in many genres. Jen and her husband live in upstate New York with their three beautiful daughters, two aloof cats and two very spoiled dogs.

Books by Jennifer D. Bokal

Harlequin Romantic Suspense

The Coltons of Kansas

Colton's Secret History

Wyoming Nights

Under the Agent's Protection

Rocky Mountain Justice

Her Rocky Mountain Hero
Her Rocky Mountain Defender
Rocky Mountain Valor

Visit the Author Profile page at Harlequin.com for more titles.

To John, you are my forever and always

Prologue

The sun had not crested over the horizon, yet the sky was lightening by degrees, from ebony to charcoal to a smoky gray. The streetlights that lined Main Street had gone dark. The stores had yet to open. The town of Braxville had yet to wake.

For Julia Jones, it was the best time of the day.

She waited in her car, the engine idling and the heat turned to full blast. A sacked lunch, packed by her mother, sat on the passenger seat. And Julia herself held a pen and notebook. The solitude was a blessing and she began—as she always did—writing a letter.

Luke,

It's been months since we last talked, but I want you to know that I love you still. I know that nei-

ther one of us can help our separation. I miss you just the same. Yesterday, I saw a commercial—the one with the cat playing the piano. Have you seen it? Do you think it's all done with computers or was the cat trained? Either way, it made me laugh. And whenever I'm happy, I think of you.

When do you think we'll be able to see each other again? I know you're busy, but I just miss you so much and would do anything to be with you right this minute.

I'll write you again tomorrow.

As always, you have all of my love,

Julia

She ripped the page from her journal. After folding it into thirds, she shoved the paper into an envelope and opened the door. Julia ran across the street, the sound of her footfalls on the pavement mingled with the *ding, ding, ding* of her car's sensor.

A blue mailbox sat on the curb. Julia set her purse atop the box as she found a pen for addressing her letter.

"Luke Walker," she wrote, before adding several hearts around his name.

From her bag, she also removed a roll of tape. A piece of tape was placed at the top of the envelope, and she stuck it to the front door of Walker Hardware. Her hand lingered on the plain white envelope as her heart raced.

"I will always love you, Luke," she said, her whispered words forming into a cloud of steam.

Her work done, Julia returned to her warm car and waited.

Like always, Luke Walker exited through the door next to the hardware store that led to several apartments. Though she'd never been invited to his house, Julia knew that Luke lived above the store—along with three other apartments he let out to rent.

Luke wore a red sweatshirt and a pair of black running shorts—an inadvisable decision given the morning's chill. Julia reached for her journal and made a note that she needed to remind Luke to dress for the weather.

Reaching his arms overhead, he twisted his torso. Left, right. Right, left. He bent at the waist and touched his toes. Slipping earbuds into his ears, Luke took the first few steps of his jog.

Julia pressed her hands to her mouth, breathless with excitement. This was the moment.

Luke stumbled to a stop. His blue eyes narrowed, his gaze directed at the letter.

He removed the envelope from the door and the paper from the envelope. Rubbing a hand on his days-old beard, he scanned the page before crumpling both in his fist. He took off at a jog once again and threw Julia's letter into a garbage can as he passed.

Her eyes filled with tears.

He'd seen her letter. He'd read it.

They were connected and he loved her still.

It wasn't the way it had been the last time, when Julia felt such a strong connection to the handsome actor in all the spy movies. She'd met Luke Walker, an important man in Braxville. Luke had taken her to the movies and to play mini-golf and out for ice cream.

Nor would this relationship end the same way it had with the actor.

Where Julia had gone to the Southern California studio, then to an agent's office, then to the actor's home. Her visit had ended when the police came and found her sitting on the kitchen floor. She was covered in blood, like hot silk, and pressed the knife to her own chest.

After that, she went to the hospital in California where days turned to weeks and weeks became months. Eventually, the scars on her wrists were nothing more than silver threads.

Her mother never said anything to anyone. Nobody in Braxville knew where she'd gone—or why.

She was home now and better than ever.

Using the side-view mirror, she watched Luke sprint down the street. Even from the back, she could tell that his blond hair was damp with sweat. His strides were long. He was taller than the actor. And sure, there were other differences—Luke's teeth weren't as straight or as white. His arms were toned, but not as well muscled as the actor's. Yet, they shared the same dark blond hair color. The same shade of eyes. The straight nose and well-defined jaw. In fact, there were so many similarities that they could be brothers.

The doctors had been right about relationships. Julia had to *personally* know someone in order to love them—and to be loved in return.

And, oh my, she did know Luke Walker. She knew his schedule. She knew how he liked to play the same game with her every morning. He'd always read her note quickly, careful to throw it away and keep their affair a secret. That was how Julia knew the two of them were fated to be together.

Moreover, Julia also knew that nothing and no one would ever keep them apart.

Chapter 1

Bridgette Colton stood in her childhood bedroom and rubbed her forehead. It wasn't yet 7:30 a.m. and a headache had started. Already, she knew her day was going to be tumultuous. Through the floorboards came the clear sound of her parents arguing.

"I see here that you've ordered thirty half-racks of ribs?" said her father, Fitz Colton, bringing the topic around to the menu for the Colton barbecue and bonfire. "Are you expecting the family or a battalion from the Kansas National Guard."

Her mother, Lilly, replied, "We have all six kids coming. Jordana and Brooks both have new romantic partners and plan to bring them. Markus Dexter and his wife, Mary, will be here. Shep is back in town. You and me. A few neighbors. Other friends. Colleagues from your work. That's a lot of people to feed, Fitz."

Her father said, "Did you see what the caterer is charging for all of this?"

"Fine," said her mother. "I'll call back and switch the order to chicken. It's only half of the price."

"Well, then we look cheap."

"You are being cheap," her mother replied, her words an arrow hitting the target.

Bridgette groaned. It was a Tuesday, the day after the October holiday and the beginning of her work week.

Beyond being back in her parents' home—and not in her apartment in Wichita—the day was far from typical. Her newest assignment as an investigator with the Kansas State Department of Health began today. She'd been tasked with discovering why so many men in Braxville had developed a rare esophageal cancer over the years.

Discovering what had caused each illness was more than finding a needle in a haystack. It was locating the right haystack in the first place.

"What do you mean we can't order a dessert?" her mother asked, Lilly's voice an octave below shrill.

Bridgette had yet to unpack her suitcase. Setting it on her unmade bed, she rummaged through her belongings until she found a bottle of OTC pain reliever. She swallowed pills without the benefit of water. As they landed in her gut, she thanked her lucky stars that she was meeting her sisters, Jordana and Yvette, for breakfast. It gave Bridgette the perfect excuse for leaving early.

Bounding down the stairs, she entered the kitchen. Her mother still wore her plaid dressing gown and sat at the long, wooden kitchen island. A mug of coffee was cupped between her hands. Standing as Bridgette entered, she set the cup aside. "Good morning, darling. You look so pretty today."

Pretty? In khakis, a cream blouse and a rust-colored cardigan, she hoped to look neat, professional, competent. Then again, her mother always had a ready compliment and Bridgette's chest filled with affection. "Thanks, Mom," she said, accepting the praise.

Her mother asked, "How did you sleep?"

"Pretty good," she said. "But I have to get going. It's a long drive into town."

"You can't leave without breakfast," said Lilly. "I'll whip up something in no time. What do you want? Pancakes? I picked up everything for French toast, if you'd like."

"Actually," said Bridgette. "I'm getting breakfast in town."

Her mother's smile faded. "Oh."

Guilt gripped Bridgette's heart and squeezed. She tried to understand her parents' situation. It was easy to imagine that with all six kids grown and gone, her mother and father had nothing to do besides ramble around in the big house and gripe at each other.

It was a problem she would fix if she could.

Then again, even if she couldn't repair her parents' marriage, she could certainly spend more time with her mother. "Hey, Mom. Can I come home at lunch tomorrow? We can look over the menu you're planning for the bonfire."

Her mother's smile returned. "I'd love that, honey."

Her father, sitting at the kitchen table, looked up from the Wichita morning paper. “Notice how she didn’t offer me pancakes or French toast?”

“That’s because you said you were on a diet,” her mother snapped. “Would you like pancakes or French toast?”

“Nope, but it would have been nice to have been asked.”

Their arguing was a constant drumbeat, and Bridgette was never going to get rid of her headache if she stayed. At thirty years of age, she really was too old to be living at home. What had she been thinking by moving in with her parents—albeit temporarily? “I really do need to get going,” she began, while reaching for her tote bag, which had been draped over the back of a chair.

“What is it that you’re doing at work?” her father asked, flicking his gaze at her from over the top of the paper.

As if she were in middle school, obedient and looking for approval, her hand grazed the strap of her bag before she let it fall to her side. Her father already knew why she was here. This was his way of getting even more information. “It’s a cancer cluster. The state thinks it’s caused by something in the environment.”

“Back in my day,” her father began, “if you got cancer it was just bad luck. Now, everyone has to blame someone, or something, for all their problems.”

“This is a rare cancer,” said Bridgette. “One that is a little more than bad luck.”

“It could be all the plastics. Your mother was telling

me we need a new washing machine with a special filter. Says all of our clothes are made from plastics and little fibers come out in the wash."

Lilly nodded. "It's horrible, Bridgette. The plastic ends up in the rivers and is eaten by the fish. Then we eat those very same fish—and the bits of plastic."

Her father harrumphed and folded the newspaper. "I say it's a hoax started by the washing machine people to fleece folks out of their hard-earned money."

Her mother countered with, "I say there is no price tag on a healthy environment."

"Okay, well, I love you both. Have a great day." She quickly grabbed her bag and turned for the door.

"Honey, you forgot these." Her mother held up a plate covered in tinfoil. "I gave you half a dozen muffins. You can share them at work."

Share muffins? Maybe her parents really did think she was still in middle school. Still, it was a sweet gesture, and everyone loves food. Arriving with a plate of homemade muffins would help Bridgette with her new coworkers. "That's very thoughtful, Mom." Placing a kiss on her mother's cheek, she continued, "I do love you both. I have to get going."

Bridgette walked from the kitchen and through the foyer. She opened the door and stepped outside, drawing in a deep breath.

She'd come back to Braxville to discover what was causing all the cases of cancer in the area and that was still her top priority. Yet, now she had a new and more immediate goal. Bridgette had to find an apartment to rent—and soon.

Thank goodness she was meeting her sisters. They both worked for the Braxville Police Department and knew the area. Hopefully, Jordana or Yvette could help. Because Bridgette knew one thing for sure—she could not stay at home.

Luke Walker stood behind the counter and stared at his computer. The screen was filled with his spreadsheet for last month's sales at Walker Hardware. The numbers didn't lie. Income was down for September, no doubt about it. What happened if the trend continued—especially since the upcoming winter months tended to be lean?

Then again, the downtown businesses were less than two weeks away from hosting the annual fall-themed Braxville Boo-fest. Last year, he made more on that single Saturday than he did the whole month.

The success spurred him to get involved, and he was the chairperson for this year's costume parade. Aside from having an event for all of Braxville to enjoy, Luke hoped to draw a crowd from Wichita, which was only an hour away. He also hoped that those from the city would make a return trip—and shop.

A knock at his front door interrupted Luke's thoughts. Stacey Navolsky, owner of the bookstore, stood outside. Hand to the glass, she peered through the window.

Tucking the tail of his flannel shirt into his jeans, Luke hustled to the door and undid the trio of locks.

"Stacey," he said, opening the door. "You're up and out early this morning."

The bookstore, like the hardware store and most every other business on Main Street—save for the coffee shop, La Dolce Vita—didn't open until 10:00 a.m. Luke hadn't looked at the clock, but it couldn't be much past eight in the morning.

Stacey was a petite woman in her fifties, with streaks of gray in her golden hair. Her typically bright blue eyes were rimmed with red. "I've had the worst night, Luke. You know how George has been sick the past few months. Well, we finally figured out what's wrong." She paused. "He has esophageal cancer."

The floor seemed to shift under Luke's feet. Memories from his youth, and of his dad's illness, came rushing back.

Gripping the doorjamb, Luke pushed away the past. "Stacey, I'm so sorry. What do the doctors say? What can I do to help out?"

"We have to go to see a specialist in Wichita next week. After that, we'll know more. As far as helping out..." Stacey paused. "I really can't chair the Boo-fest anymore. I was thinking about posting on social media and asking someone to step up. But I wanted to speak with you first to see if you're able and interested. People like you, Luke. They trust you. You're a natural leader."

Luke interrupted, "I appreciate all your praise, but you don't have to butter me up, Stacey. I'll take over as the chairperson. Besides, you have bigger things to worry about than a downtown festival."

"Are you sure?"

"Positive," said Luke. His head began to ache. He needed a double shot of espresso. Then again, cash flow was down, and he didn't want to spend money he didn't have. "I've got everything under control."

"Here," Stacey said, and withdrew a large, three-ring binder from a canvas bag she had draped over her shoulder. "This is the outline of everything I've done so far."

Luke accepted the heavy tome, realizing too late that he'd taken on a bigger job than imagined. Maybe, just this once, he'd splurge on a coffee. He didn't know how he'd get through all the information without one. "Thanks," he said, flipping through the first few pages. "This looks very thorough."

"Well, I better get going," said Stacey.

"Absolutely." Luke walked with her, pulling the door opcn. "Give George my best. Again, if you need anything, let me know."

"You're doing more than enough," she said. Rising to tiptoe, she placed a small kiss on his cheek. "You are a great guy, Luke Walker. I hope some smart woman snatches you up—and quick."

At thirty-one years of age, Luke heard comments about his bachelorhood all the time. It wasn't that he wanted to be perpetually single. He had yet to find the right woman.

Stepping out onto the street, Stacey gave one last wave before turning toward her bookstore.

Luke followed and remained on the sidewalk. A breeze blew, sending a piece of paper skittering down the street. He picked up the rubbish and placed it in a bin. Gooseflesh rose on his arms and it wasn't just from the weather.

Luke felt a tickling at the back of his neck, just a

whisper of pressure, as if he were being watched—and he knew by whom.

Casting a glance over his shoulder, he searched for the ever-present dark blue sedan. It was there, just as he knew it would be, parked across the street. The pale face of his ex-girlfriend, Julia, was unmistakable in the driver's seat.

Maybe the term ex-girlfriend was a little too generous for their relationship. Luke had dated her briefly over the summer. They'd had no more than half a dozen dates before he ended the relationship.

Soon after, she started watching the store and his apartment upstairs. At first he tried being honest—telling Julia that their romance was not meant to be.

She disagreed.

He blocked her phone when she continued to call and text.

He blocked her again when she changed her number.

He threatened to contact the police—something he never intended to do.

His warning changed nothing.

He threw away the letters she left in the morning and vowed to never look in her direction.

Eventually, she'd get bored, right?

So far she hadn't.

Without another glance in Julia's direction, Luke stepped back into the store. Despite his need for coffee, he didn't want to cross the street and risk a confrontation with Julia. Taking his time, he re-engaged all three locks.

What had started as a long day had just become a lot longer. Then again, Luke wasn't the kind to complain.

He was invested in Braxville's success as more than a business owner, being a lifetime resident, as well. So, yeah, there wasn't much of anything he wasn't willing to do—even become the last-minute chairperson of the festival—for his hometown.

Bridgette pulled her car next to the curb, taking a spot behind a blue sedan. Main Street in Braxville was like walking into a page from a history book—coming from a time when life was simple or at least seemed that way. The street was lined on both sides with small shops and restaurants. Most were built of brick, pressing cheek to jowl with one another and only rising three stories from the ground. Glass storefronts gleamed in the morning sun, and light posts of wrought iron stood on every corner.

It was hard not to smile.

After stepping onto the sidewalk, she strode up Main Street and cast a glance at the blue sedan. A dark-haired woman gripped the steering wheel with knuckles gone white. Her gaze was locked on the front door of the hardware store.

The woman took no note of Bridgette, yet her stare left Bridgette walking a bit faster.

Walker Hardware. Now that was a place Bridgette hadn't thought of in years.

While growing up, the dad of her friend had owned Walker Hardware.

For a moment, she wondered what had become of

Luke Walker. Was he still in Braxville? Or was he just another ghost from her past that haunted her still?

Pulling open the door to La Dolce Vita, she was greeted with the earthy scent of roasting coffee beans. Several round tables filled the center of the room. A glass-and-chrome pastry case separated the restaurant from the area where coffees and other beverages were prepared. Her older sister, Jordana, a detective with the Braxville Police Department, already sat at a table near the window.

She stood as Bridgette approached and pulled her in for a big hug. "How are you? I'm so glad that you're home."

"It's good to see you," said Bridgette, embracing her sister in return. Jordana was as tall as Bridgette, five feet nine inches. Her older sister wore her hair in a loose bun and had donned a long jacket in olive green that brought out the auburn highlights in her hair. Years ago, Bridgette learned that Jordana's clothing choices had nothing to do with fashion and all to do with function. Without a doubt, the jacket had been chosen to cover her sister's sidearm. Bridgette continued, "Then again, I'm not sure that I'm actually happy to be back. It's been a rough morning already. Do Mom and Dad get along at all?"

"No," said Jordana honestly. She returned to her seat. "They fight constantly. It's a bit tiring."

"A bit?" Bridgette asked with mock incredulity, while sitting across from her sister. "Can I be candid? I don't think that I can stay at the house while I'm in town. Do you know of any place I can rent?"

"Rent? Be serious. You can live with me. Clint is around a lot, but you'll really like him."

"Live with you and your new boyfriend? No, thank you. I'd rather stay with Mom and Dad." She winked to show that she was teasing, yet the last thing Bridgette wanted was to interrupt her sister's newest romance.

"Sorry I can't be more helpful, but I really can't think of any place on the market." Jordana paused. "Maybe Yvette knows some place that's available."

"Speaking of Yvette," said Bridgette. "Where is our baby sister?"

"She's running late. There's a big case."

"What happened?"

Before Jordana could answer, a server arrived with two cups of coffee and chocolate croissants. "I took the liberty of ordering for you," said Jordana. "I hope your tastes haven't changed while living in the big city."

"There's nothing better than Megan Parker's pastries," she said, mentioning the coffee shop's owner. After taking a big bite, Bridgette continued, "Besides, my tastes haven't changed at all. I live in Wichita, not on the moon."

"And how is life? Really?"

Bridgette knew what Jordana was asking. It had been nearly two years since Bridgette's husband, Henry, died in a car accident. The food turned to sand in her mouth, and she washed it down with a swallow of coffee. "Work is good," she said.

"There's more to life than work."

"I belong to two book clubs," said Bridgette. "I attend a yoga class three times a week and volunteer at the local dog shelter every other Saturday. I have a life, thank you very much."

"Anyone cute at the dog shelter?"

"There is this adorable lab-mix, but he was adopted last month." Bridgette took another bite.

"Har-har," said Jordana. "Anyone cute who walks on two legs? Preferably a human."

"None that I've seen."

"Have you even bothered to look?"

"Honestly," said Bridgette. "No. And before you try to get all big sister on me and boss me into having a relationship, I'm not good at romance. Period. End of story."

Jordana reached for Bridgette's wrist and squeezed lightly. "You are too young to give up on love. Henry was a great guy. We all thought so and we all miss him, too. He's gone and that's tragic, but I don't want to see you alone for the rest of your life."

"That's the point," said Bridgette. She pulled her arm away and reached for a napkin. After wiping her mouth, she continued, "It's my life."

Jordana lifted a hand in surrender. "I get it. I'll back off."

"You get what?" Yvette asked, standing next to the table. Yvette had the same dark hair and eyes as Jordana, but the similarities ended there. Then again, Bridgette was a triplet and she looked nothing like her brothers, Brooks and Neil. Yvette continued, "What'd I miss?"

Standing, Bridgette embraced her baby sister. "Nothing, really," she said, not wanting to share the almost quarrel with Jordana. Bridgette didn't know what she would do if both of her sisters teamed up and tried to force a new man into her life.

"Mom and Dad argue too much," said the eldest Colton daughter. She stood and hugged Yvette. "Bridgette's looking for an apartment. Know of anything?"

"I might, actually," said Yvette. They all took their seats. "Let me talk to a few people and get back to you."

"Thanks so much," said Bridgette. She took another bite of her pastry. "Jordana said that you're working a big case. What happened?"

Yvette gave their older sister an unmistakable side-eye. "We really aren't supposed to talk about work, but two bodies were found in the walls of a building that Dad's company is renovating."

Bridgette choked on her coffee. "What?" She spluttered. "Never mind. I might be a Colton, but I'm not a cop." She glanced at her smart watch. It was 8:20 a.m. "Shoot, I didn't realize that it was so late. I need to scram. How much do I owe for breakfast?"

"It's on me," said Jordana.

Bridgette didn't have time to argue with her sister. "I'll treat next time," she said, while grabbing her bag and heading for the door. Luckily, Bridgette's temporary office was located in City Hall and only blocks from where she had parked her car. If she hurried, she could go back to her auto and grab the plate of muffins her mother had prepared. That would help smooth over any rough edges a minute of tardiness might cause.

As she hurried down the street, Bridgette marveled that the Braxville of her childhood had changed very little. Yet, it seemed as if the quaint downtown, the tree-lined streets and the well-kept homes were little more than a facade.

There were bodies buried in walls. Clusters of cancer cases. And the woman from before still sat in her car and stared across the street.

Despite the charm of her hometown, Bridgette knew that Braxville was hiding the answer to more than one mystery.

Chapter 2

The Kansas State Department of Health had set up their temporary office in City Hall, located across the street from the town park and only a few blocks from the coffee shop where Bridgette had parked her car.

She took the stairs to the second floor and found the suite of rooms assigned to the DOH at the back at the building. Juggling her bag and the plate, Bridgette pushed the door open with her hip. A round clock hung on the wall. Not only was she on time for work, she had made it with four minutes to spare.

The office was a single room with several workstations around the perimeter. A large conference table sat in the middle of the space. A dry-erase board filled half of one wall. On it was a list of names. Several windows overlooked the back street and Bridgette could see the roof of her father's office, Colton Construction, in the distance.

Two men, at separate workstations, held phones to their ears. A single woman sat at the table. A pile of folders was stacked at her elbow. She looked up as Bridgette crossed the threshold.

Holding up the plate of muffins, Bridgette said, "Morning, folks. I brought food."

The woman stood. "Welcome. You must be Bridgette Colton. I'm Rachel Shaw, I went to school with your brother, Tyler." She pointed to one of the men, an African American with a goatee, "That's Adam Stevens and the other guy is Carson Mathews."

Carson wore a short-sleeved shirt covered in a tropical print. He turned his seat. With the phone still to his ear, he waved and mouthed, *Good morning.*

Adam ended his call and moved to the table. "Food?"

Bridgette set the plate down and removed the foil. "Homemade muffins," she said. "Help yourself."

Adam took a bite. "You are quite the cook."

"Thanks," said Bridgette. "I'm staying with my parents until I find an apartment in town, so they're compliments of my mother."

"Good job, Mrs. Colton," said Adam, finishing his last bit.

Carson ended the call. He moved to the table and took a muffin from the plate. "Nice to meet you."

Bridgette made a mental note to thank her mother. Lilly had been right—food had helped to make inroads with her new coworkers. "Since we're all here," she began, taking a seat at the table, "let's get started."

For the next twenty minutes, Bridgette was briefed about the cancer clusters. In short, a study showed that twenty years ago, six men had developed esophageal cancer. Two died, and four were either in remission or struggling with the cancer's return. Then, more recently, another group of men had been diagnosed with the same exact cancer.

"What are your thoughts?" Bridgette asked.

"It's too specific to be random," said Adam, helping himself to another muffin.

"So, it's not bad luck," said Bridgette, echoing her father's earlier sentiment.

"No way," said Rachel. "It has to be environmental. The men aren't related."

"Smokers?" Bridgette asked. "Other tobacco use? Are they all heavy drinkers?"

"Two men from the first group smoked more than a pack of cigarettes each day," said Carson. "No other tobacco use is listed. A few admitted to regularly consuming more than three drinks a night before becoming ill. If this was caused by alcohol or tobacco, why aren't more people sick?"

"That's a good point," said Bridgette. She rose to her feet and walked to the dry-erase board. "Are these all the cases?"

"It's everyone we have so far," Adam said. "The original names are on the left. The newly diagnosed patients are on the right."

Bridgette scanned the list of names. Her gaze stopped on a name she knew from her childhood.

Ernest O'Rourke.

For years, he had been her father's foreman.

Bridgette asked, "Do you have contact information for all of the men?"

"Sure do," said Rachel. She pulled the pile of folders toward her seat.

"Can you find this one?" asked Bridgette, pointing to Ernest's name.

Rachel flipped through the files. "Here you go," she said, holding out a manila folder.

Bridgette looked at the information. The address was still the same. For a moment, she was transported to years before. She was sitting on the bench seat of her father's truck. A meal, prepared and packed by her mother, sat between them.

Her father tapped the steering wheel, keeping time with the latest song on the country station. At the chorus, both father and daughter bellowed the words. As the song ended, Bridgette dissolved into peals of laughter. For her, it had been one of the few perfect moments spent with her father.

What if there was more than she remembered or more than she'd been told?

Had Ernest been sick then? Was that why they were delivering food?

"I'm going to start with this case," she said, holding up the file. "In fact, I'll interview him right now."

"Now?" echoed Adam. "We usually make an appointment first. Otherwise, we don't know if the patient has time—or the inclination—to speak with us."

What Adam said was entirely true—and DOH policy. "Ernest O'Rourke will have time for me."

"How can you be so confident?" asked Rachel.

"Because," said Bridgette, "I've known him my whole life." Lifting her bag from the floor, she slipped the file inside. "I'll be back in a few hours."

Bridgette walked back to the ground floor and started up the street toward her car but slowed her gait. Just like it had been when she arrived, the blue sedan was still parked at the curb. The same woman still sat in the driver's seat and continued to watch the hardware store. The woman's intense gaze left Bridgette feeling as if she'd been grabbed by an icy hand, and a shiver ran down her spine.

For the second time in a single morning, a knock on the store's front door interrupted Luke's pre-opening routine. He looked up. Standing on the sidewalk, Yvette Colton waved.

Luke hustled to open the door. "Hey, stranger," he said. "I haven't seen you in months. Is there anything I can help you find?"

"Do you still own all those rental properties?" she asked. "I know someone who needs a place temporarily—for a month or two."

"I sure do," he said. "When would they need the place?"

"Soon," Yvette said. "Like today, if possible."

Today? Aside from the hardware store on the ground floor, Luke owned the whole building, including the two floors above. Over the years, he had renovated the space into four apartments, two on each level. "There's one apartment open," he said. "Right across the hall from me. You're in luck, the last tenant moved out over the summer. It's been freshly painted and comes fully furnished."

"Sounds perfect," said Yvette. "Can we see it at lunchtime?"

Luke paused. The noon hour was one of the busiest for the store. Did he really want to risk losing customers by closing down at lunch? Then again, filling the vacant apartment would help make ends meet. Moving to the counter, he found a set of keys along with a copy of a boilerplate lease he always used. Sliding the keys and lease toward Yvette, he asked, "Can you show the apartment? If your friend likes it, they can just sign and bring me this copy later today."

"Are you sure you don't want to meet the new renter?"

"I've known you your whole life. If they come with your recommendation, then that's good enough for me." Yvette took the keys and paperwork while Luke continued, "Take the door to the left of the store. Second floor, apartment 2A. Only door on the right."

"Thanks, Luke. I'll keep you posted."

Yvette pushed the door open, passing a newly retired homeowner as she left.

"Glad to see that you've opened early," said the older man. "The missus just told me that we have company coming for Thanksgiving. She gave me a honey-do list longer than my arm."

The store didn't officially open for another half hour. Yet, Luke wasn't going to quibble about time. The day had started, promising nothing but problems, and in short order it had turned around.

"Show me that list," said Luke to the customer. "Let's see what you need."

He led the older man down the paint aisle and wondered about the possible tenant. Should he meet with whoever Yvette Colton brought to the apartment? After all they would be a renter, and his neighbor, as well.

There were other thoughts that were harder to shake. It was impossible to see anyone from the Colton clan without thinking of his long-ago school buddy, Bridgette. Then again, Bridgette had been more than his friend. The summer between high school and college, she had been his first love—his first lover.

At the time, he had hoped their relationship was more than a fleeting romance.

He'd been wrong. Bridgette went to college. A few years later, he heard that she was getting married. Then later came the news that Bridgette had been widowed.

As he explained all the choices for interior paint, Luke couldn't help wondering what had happened to Bridgette Colton?

Bridgette knew the way to Ernest O'Rourke's house by heart and had no need to use her GPS for directions. The brick ranch seemed smaller than she recalled. Then again, the last time she was here, Bridgette was a kid and so her perspective had changed. The trim around the door and windows were in need of a coat of paint, and a carpet of leaves covered the yard.

She stepped from the car and slammed the door shut.

After grabbing her bag from the back seat, she turned to the house.

"Beautiful Bridgette Colton," a voice boomed. Ernest stood on the threshold. Like the house, he was smaller than she remembered. This time, it wasn't just her memory. The once robust foreman was stooped and shriveled. He continued, "I recognized you the minute you pulled onto the street."

"Hi, Ernest," she said. "It's good to see you."

"What did I do to get a visit from my favorite Colton?"

While striding up the walkway, she said, "I should've called before stopping by, but your name came up with work." She paused, not sure what to say next. Lifting her bag higher on her shoulder, she continued, "Here I am."

"You don't need to call, you know that." Turning for the house, he gestured for Bridgette to follow. "Come in. I'm happy to help you with whatever I can."

The welcome was more than Bridgette had hoped to get. Ernest led her to the kitchen and pointed to a round wooden table. "Have a seat. Can I pour you a cup of coffee? Do you want a cup of tea?"

One professional rule that Bridgette kept as sacrosanct was to always accept any hospitality offered by a person involved in a study. Despite the fact that she wasn't thirsty, she said, "A cup of tea would be nice."

Ernest filled a kettle with water from the tap and placed it on the stove. "Won't take a minute to boil," he said, sitting in a chair across from Bridgette. "How's your mom and your dad?" he asked.

The argument from earlier came to mind. "Good," she lied. "Same as always."

"Now, you said that my name came up in connection with your job. How'd that happen?"

Bridgette had set her bag on the floor, next to her feet. She reached for the folder and set it on the table. "I'm in Braxville to look into a cluster of cancer cases."

Ernest sat back in his seat hard, as if she'd kicked him in the gut. His face turned the color of used paste. "Esophageal cancer, I bet," he said.

Bridgette nodded just as the whistle on the teakettle let out a long, shrill blast. "Let me get that," she said, rising to her feet. Mugs were already placed on the stove. A canister set lined the back of the counter. One of them said *tea.* It took her only a moment to prepare a cup for each of them.

"Here you go," she said, setting a steaming mug in front of Ernest.

Wrapping his hands around the cup, he asked, "Can I ask you a question?"

"Of course."

"I had cancer two decades ago. Why are people interested now?"

Bridgette blew on the tea before taking a sip. "Cancer of all kinds is to be expected in any given community. When there are more cases than anticipated, it's considered a cluster. The DOH has mapped out nearly a dozen cases in Braxville. You are in the first group, those from twenty years ago. There is another group that has formed more recently and that's what makes us nervous."

"Why's that?" Ernest asked, giving Bridgette time to collect her thoughts.

"Simply put, it means there's something causing everyone to get sick."

"You don't say," said Ernest. "We used to joke—Tom, Bill and me—that working with your dad was what gave us cancer."

Cup halfway to her mouth, Bridgette froze. "What'd you say?"

"Back when I worked for your dad, two other guys on our crew got sick at the same time as me."

Setting her cup aside, Bridgette withdrew a pad of paper and a pen from her bag. "Bill? Tom?"

"Bill Warner and Tom Cromwell."

Bridgette wrote down the names. She had yet to commit all the men from the cluster to memory but knew that these names were already on the list. "Do you keep in touch with Bill and Tom?"

"They both passed away." Ernest stared at the cup in his hands and shook his head. "The cancer took Tom about eighteen years ago. Bill had a heart attack four years back. So, his death wasn't cancer related. Then again, Bill was always sick after what he went through." He took a sip of tea and set the cup back on the table.

"It sounds like you knew both of the men well."

"We grew up together. Went to school from kindergarten to graduation. We hunted in the fall. Fished in the summer. I got them both jobs at Colton Construction."

Bridgette placed a hand on the older man's arm. His skin was dry and paper-thin. "Can I ask you some questions? If not now, I can make an appointment and come back."

"I hope you come and visit an old man while you work in Braxville, but I have nothing else to do right now. Ask away."

Tapping her pen on the pad, Bridgette wondered what question was most pertinent. Her mother's desire for a new washing machine with a filter came to mind. As did the report that plastic ends up in the river, where filaments were ingested by the fish. And then the fish eaten by humans. There was no scientific evidence linking the plastics to cancer, but it did bring up an interesting question. What else might be in the water?

"Do you still fish a lot?"

"Whenever I get the chance."

"You always catch something?"

"I'd be a poor fisherman if I didn't."

"How often do you eat what you catch?"

"Never," said Ernest. "I'm a catch-and-release kind of guy."

Still, it would be prudent to test the river's water. She made a note.

"Have you ever smoked, Ernest?"

"As a teenager, sure. Everyone did."

"I have a few questions and I want you to think back to your life before you were diagnosed with cancer when answering."

"Got it."

Bridgette had a long-practiced set of questions she asked everyone involved in an investigation. She began by asking, "Did you ever drink excessive alcohol? Take drugs not prescribed by a doctor? Finally, how would you describe your exercise routine?"

"Did I ever get drunk as a young man? Sure," said Ernest with a shrug. "In fact, most every Friday we'd all go out and have one too many after work. Take drugs not prescribed a doctor—never. In fact, I didn't go to the doctor regular-like before I got sick. Now, I have to go twice a year, whether I think I need to be there or not. And exercise? I can't say I was ever a runner or a gym rat. I carried roofing tiles up and down ladders for a living, so I'd say that counts as being fit."

"I'd say you're right," said Bridgette, copying Ernest's statement, word for word. Before she got a chance to ask her next question, her phone pinged with an incoming text. She glanced at the screen. It was from Yvette. Bridgette wasn't about to interrupt an initial interview to reply to her sister. Silencing her phone, she returned to her list of questions for Ernest.

By the time she was through, Bridgette had taken over ten pages of notes and drunk three cups of tea. Her first morning of working in Braxville was almost gone.

After asking her last set of questions, Bridgette rose to her feet and placed her notepad and pen into her bag. "Thanks for taking the time to speak to me, Ernest. I appreciate it. Will you call if you think of anything else?"

"Only if you promise to come out and visit again."

"Of course," said Bridgette, giving the older man a hug.

Walking back to her car, Bridgette fished her phone from her bag and read the text from Yvette. I found a place. Fully furnished. In downtown Braxville. I can show you today at lunch.

Bridgette sent her sister a reply. You're the best. Meet in 1 hour?

Yvette replied with a thumbs-up emoji and an address on Main Street.

With her problem of housing hopefully solved, she focused on what she'd learned from Ernest. There was something he said that bothered her more than she'd let on. Three of her father's employees had esophageal cancer. She didn't have time to do the math, but she knew the odds of that being a coincidence were pretty lousy. Could there really be a connection between the men who developed cancer and Colton Construction?

Chapter 3

Bridgette still had an hour until meeting her sister to look at the apartment. With time to spare, she drove to the offices of Colton Construction. Her father's large white pickup was parked in a reserved place next to the front door. She maneuvered her car into a spot several rows back and turned off the engine.

Walking to the front door, Bridgette couldn't help but marvel at the business her father had built. When she was a child, it had been a family-run operation—dad and grandpa building houses. Decades earlier, the old office had been a single trailer—drafty in the winter and sweltering in the summer. Grandpa kept lollipops on hand in case any of the Colton kids stopped by.

Now the offices had a metal roof of cobalt blue. The glass-and-brick building sat on the same dusty parcel of land at the edge of town, but now took up over 10,000 square feet. Behind the office were several outbuildings. The original trailer had been converted to a mail room. There was a warehouse as large as an airplane hangar. A garage held the fleet of construction equipment. The staff had grown, as well. What started as two men and a handful of full-time employees had grown to a full office staff, dozens of construction workers, plumbers and electricians. Her father had even hired a full-time architect and planned to expand by bringing a civil engineer onto the staff, as well.

Business was definitely good for Colton Construction.

Pulling open the front door, Bridgette couldn't help wondering what her grandfather would think of all the progress. Would he be proud? Or would he not see the expansion as an improvement?

A receptionist sat behind a large glass desk and looked up as Bridgette entered. "Can I help you?" the woman asked.

How long had it been since she'd visited her father at work? Long enough that Colton Construction had a new receptionist. "I need to speak to Fitzpatrick Colton."

"Can I tell him what this is regarding?"

"I'm Bridgette," she said. "His daughter."

The woman blushed slightly. "Your father mentioned that you were back in town. It's nice to meet you."

Bridgette smiled. "It's nice to meet you, too. And my dad, is he available?"

"You can go right on back."

After thanking the receptionist, Bridgette found the office.

Her father sat behind a large wooden desk. He wore a quarter-zip sweater over a golf shirt. Pen tapping on his bottom lip, Bridgette's dad leaned back in a leather desk chair. Her dad's partner, Markus Dexter—otherwise known as Uncle Dex—wore a gray blazer and a pristine white shirt open at the collar. He was situated in an armchair across the desk from Fitz Colton. The two men looked up, glaring, as she entered.

Bridgette had no idea what they'd been discussing, but the tension was palpable, almost a physical thing.

Tripping to a stop, she paused on the threshold. "Morning, Daddy. I need your help. Is now a bad time?"

"It's never a bad time to see you," said Dex, while rising to his feet. He placed a kiss on her cheek. "I'll let you and your dad catch up. Fitz, we can talk later."

"See you at the bonfire on Friday," said Bridgette.

"I heard your mom is serving ribs," said Dex. "I wouldn't miss it for the world."

She waited until Dex was gone before dropping into the chair he had just vacated. "Is everything okay? You and Uncle Dex seemed upset."

Her father waved away her question. "There's a police matter at a site we're renovating for the city. It's never good if the police are involved."

Bridgette recalled her sisters mentioning just such an issue this morning. She struggled with what, if anything, to say. In the end, she decided on discretion and said nothing. "I saw Ernest O'Rourke this morning."

A look passed over her father's face. What had it been?

Surprise? Sure, but there'd been more. What was it? Hurt? Anger?

In the end, she decided it was a look of regret. It was gone as quickly as it came, and Bridgette wasn't positive that she'd seen anything at all.

"How's Ernest these days?" her father asked. "I haven't seen much of him since he retired a few years back."

"Did you know that he had esophageal cancer two decades ago?"

"Sure," said her dad. "It was awful. Your mother and I were torn up over his illness. He wasn't able to work for a few months while getting treatment. Of course, Ernest is a tough old bird and he kicked the cancer in the nuts—excuse my language—and came back, good as new."

"He said that two other employees of Colton Construction had the same illness at roughly the same time."

Her father shook his head, "I don't think so. I would've remembered something like that. Must be that Ernest is mistaken."

"He was really good friends with these men." She removed the notebook from her bag, scanning her notes for the names. "Bill Warner and Tom Cromwell. Do you remember them?"

"Can't say that either of those names ring a bell for me," said her father. "But that was a long time ago. People come and go in the construction business, you know that."

"Ernest said they grew up together and he was the one who got them both jobs." She paused and chewed on her bottom lip. How could she ask her father the next question without being rude? She knew the answer—there was no way to bring up the subject without being impertinent. Then again, she was doing her job—her relationship with the company notwithstanding. "Any chance that the men were exposed to carcinogens on the job?"

"You think the men got cancer from working for me?" Her father poked the top of his desk with his pen. "Bill Warner was a large guy with a heart condition who never exercised. In fact, he would rather eat a dozen doughnuts than look at an apple. Tom Cromwell was the reason the phrase *smoked like a freight train* was invented. I don't know what happened to Ernest, but neither of those other men were overly healthy when they worked for me." Tossing the pen onto the desk, her father continued, "And I always made sure those boys had health insurance, even if they couldn't work."

"I thought you said that you didn't remember either Bill or Tom."

Her father sat back in his seat, his eyes wide. "I don't," he began. "Or rather, I didn't. Then when you mentioned that they were good friends with Ernest and grew up together, I knew who you were talking about. I just didn't remember their names at first."

Her father's answer made complete sense. If that was the case, though, why had a hard knot dropped into her middle? "Is there any chance I can get employee records to cross-reference with all the other names I have on the list?"

"From twenty years back?" Her father scratched the back of his head. "Sweetie, I'd love to help you out with your job, but I don't think I've kept any records that go back that far. I'm sorry."

Before Bridgette could say anything else, her phone started to ring. She glanced at the screen. It was her baby sister and—what's more—Bridgette was late. "I have to go," she said. "I'm meeting Yvette downtown."

"Go," said Fitz. "I'll see you at home tonight, okay?"

The phone quit ringing as the call went to voice mail. "I'm not sure about that, Daddy. I'm looking at getting my own place. I love you and Mom, but—"

Her father interrupted, "You're thirty years old and living with your parents is sad."

"I'm glad you understand," she said. Her phone started to ring again. It was Yvette, blowing up her cell.

"Your mother will be disappointed," said her father.

"I know," said Bridgette. "I don't want to hurt her feelings."

"Let me talk to her. She seems to be upset with me all the time, so I can handle a little more heat from your mother."

"You're the best, Daddy," said Bridgette. While swiping the call open, she turned from her father's office and retraced her steps toward the reception area. To Yvette, she said, "I'm on my way. Sorry to be late."

While rushing to her car, Bridgette wished she had time for a leisurely drive or a long walk. She felt as if she had learned important information during the morning. It was as if she'd been given only a few pieces of a puzzle, and without time to think, she'd never be able to see how everything fit together.

Bridgette made the return trip to Braxville in record time. She found a parking place at the curb, next to the address provided by Yvette's text. It was near where she had parked earlier in the day. Stepping from her car, she looked for the blue sedan along with the driver and her intense and chilling stare.

The woman and her car were gone.

Thick gray clouds rolled across the sky and sun. It seemed as if the vibrant colors had been leached from Braxville and the town had been reset in tones of sepia. Yvette stood in front of the hardware store with her arms folded across her chest against the gathering chill. She wore a bright red scarf around her neck. The color made her brown eyes appear a shade darker.

"Don't you look stylish," said Bridgette, almost teasing. "Anyone in particular you want to impress?"

"Can't a girl just want to look good for herself? Does my appearance have to be about a guy?"

In Bridgette's estimation, it almost always had something to do with a man. Yet, her sister was right. Yvette was entitled to look good for herself. "You said there was an apartment for rent? What are we doing at the hardware store?"

"It's above the store. Owned by the store's owner," said Yvette, while working a key into an adjacent door's lock.

The store's owner? When Bridgette was in high

school, that had been Luke's dad, Paul. How would she feel about renting a place from her old boyfriend's father? Could things get worse than living at home?

As Yvette pulled the door open, Bridgette asked, "Does Paul still own Walker Hardware?"

"Paul?" she echoed with a shake of her head. "No, the owner isn't named Paul."

Bridgette didn't press for more information—like what happened to Paul Walker. Or if his son was still in town. And if Luke was around, was he married? Or happy? Did he ever wonder about Bridgette, or why she slipped quietly from his life—and his mind—forever?

The door from the street led to a narrow landing, with a bank of mailboxes on the wall. There was also a set of stairs that led upward. The steps were clean. There were no odd odors hanging in the air.

As they climbed the first flight, Bridgette couldn't help being hopeful.

"Let's see," said Yvette as they reached the landing. "He said it was apartment 2A, on the right. That's this one." She had another key, for another lock. Opening the door with a flourish, she said, "Voilà!"

Bridgette stepped inside and smiled. The floors were wooden. The living room was furnished with a sofa, chair and coffee table. The kitchen had enough room for a small table. High windows overlooked Main Street, and from where she stood she could see La Dolce Vita.

Pointing to the coffee shop, Bridgette said, "Next time we meet, you can just wave when you arrive."

"Or I can get takeout and come up to your place."

"Even better." There was a single door off the living room that led to a master suite. Bed. Dresser. Chest of drawers. The closet was small, but she'd survive. A bathroom was set off the bedroom. Shower, tub, sink. It was everything she wanted—and more.

"It's perfect," she said. "I'll take it."

"You can think about it, maybe negotiate for a lower rent since this place has been vacant for a few months," said Yvette.

"I've thought about it enough," she said. "And I'd pay extra to get out of Mom and Dad's house. I love them both, you know."

"They don't get along and their fighting makes everyone miserable," Yvette finished for her. "Don't forget, I'm the baby. I had to stay at home after everyone went to college."

"I'm glad you understand," said Bridgette. "I hope Mom does, too."

"Well, if you're sure you want the apartment, I have a copy of the lease." Yvette held up several sheets of paper.

Bridgette scanned the information. The rent was low in comparison to what she paid in Wichita, but still top dollar for Braxville. On the final page she found a line for her signature. After signing, she wrote a check for the first month's rent. Handing both to her sister, she said, "If your job as a crime scene investigator doesn't work out, you might have a future in real estate."

"Thanks," she said. "I'm going to deliver this to the owner now. If you want, I'll introduce you to your new landlord and neighbor."

Bridgette consulted her phone for the time. It was

one thirty. "I'd love to, but I've been out of the office all morning. I better get back." She added, "Thanks for finding me an apartment."

"What are little sisters for?"

"Aside from rummaging through my closet, you mean?"

"Hey, that was a long time ago. But I am excited to see what all you've brought with you. I haven't decided what to wear to the bonfire this weekend."

After giving her sister a quick hug, Bridgette left her new home.

Now that Bridgette had her own place, she could focus on her job. It was odd that three men, close friends since childhood, ended up developing the same cancer. Certainly, they had much more in common than working for her father's company. It would take all of Bridgette's investigative skills to figure out what it was.

Jogging down the stairs, she opened the door leading to the sidewalk and stepped outside. The gathering clouds had darkened, and the wind held a chill. She predicted rain tonight. After buttoning up her jacket, she glanced into the window of Walker Hardware. Her reflection was superimposed on the glass, and the store was filled with people. Her mouth went dry as she scanned the crowd.

He wouldn't be there, she knew. Why then, was Bridgette looking for her old love, Luke Walker?

What started as a lousy day had turned around for Luke Walker. The hardware store had been busy. During the midday rush, Yvette Colton delivered a signed lease for the apartment upstairs—along with a check for the first month's rent. He hadn't had time to look at either.

After the store closed, he turned off the lights and left through the main entrance. While locking the door, a tickling ran up his spine. He'd become accustomed to the sensation. Still, the hairs at the nape of his neck stood on end. Using the front window as a mirror, he glanced over his shoulder.

Just as he expected, Julia, his ex-girlfriend, stood across the street. Streetlamps shone on every corner, bathing downtown Braxville in a golden glow. By mid-block, the darkness took over and left everything in shadow.

Julia stood in one of the dark places. Luke wasn't sure if it was a trick of the light or the distortion of the glass, but it looked as if Julia had no eyes—just empty, black sockets. He swallowed. Maybe his decision not to involve the police had been too hasty.

The apartment building was next to the hardware store. With the feeling of Julia's sightless gaze still on his back, Luke fumbled with the keys as he unlocked the dead bolt. After stepping inside, he shoved the door closed with a *crack*.

The uneasy feeling slipped away as he climbed the stairs. On the landing, he paused. The softly crooning voice of a country-and-western singer came from inside the newly rented apartment. It was six thirty and not an unreasonable time to visit—especially since he owned the building.

Lifting his hand, Luke rapped his knuckles on the

wooden door. From inside, he heard the sound of footsteps and a woman's voice. "Just a second."

The door opened.

For Luke, time stopped. His pulse began to race, filling his skull with the *whomp, whomp* of rushing blood.

He shook away the numbness.

Of course, it all made sense. Yvette Colton coming to him. A tenant who needed a place for a few months. It's just that Luke never would have guessed, although he probably should have known.

"Bridgette," he said. For the first time in ages, he smiled, and the expression wasn't forced. "Wow. I mean, I didn't expect you to have rented the apartment." He still held the envelope with the lease and the check, realizing only moments too late that he should have taken the time to at least glance at both before knocking on the door.

She lifted one eyebrow. "Luke Walker. What in the world are you doing here? Yvette said your dad sold the hardware store years ago."

It was hard to miss the ice in Bridgette's tone. Sure, it had been years since they had last spoken. Their final conversation had been cordial, if not friendly. She had called to say hello. His father was sick. Luke was worried that his dad's cancer had returned. Bridgette had listened and then disappeared from his life.

"My dad did sell the store—to me," he said in answer to her question. "And then I bought the rest of the building, too."

"You're my landlord?" she asked, her question dripping with incredulity. "This isn't going to work, Luke."

"What won't work? You can't rent an apartment from me for a few months?" Then again, it had been years. A lot had changcd. Through distancc and timc, whatever feelings they once had for each other were gone.

"You know what?" he said, holding out the envelope that held the lease and Bridgette's check. "Yvette dropped this off at the store. You can have your money back and tear up the rental agreement. I'm not sure why we're enemies, but I'm too old for any idiocy from high school."

Outside, rain started to fall. A thousand tiny arrows hitting the windowpane.

Bridgette dropped her gaze and chewed on her bottom lip. "You're right, Luke. Whatever happened between us is ancient history. I guess I was surprised to see you, that's all."

"It seems like finding me on your doorstep was more than an unpleasant surprise. I really don't want you to stay if I make you uncomfortable."

"Are you kicking me out?"

"Of course not," he said before considering her question.

"Can I apologize for being rude? Is there any way we can start over?"

Bridgette's hostile reaction had stung, but Luke wasn't the kind to hold a grudge, and he found himself saying, "Sure. Of course."

"Thanks," said Bridgette, giving him that same smile she always had—the one that sent his heartbeat racing and left his palms damp.

Chapter 4

Bridgette placed her hand on the closed wooden door, her heartbeat racing. In all honesty she never thought she'd see Luke again, much less find him living across the hallway. Then again Braxville was a small town, and she had to be prepared to see people from her childhood.

Yet, could Luke really be living across the hall?

Despite the fact that she knew it to be true, it was all unbelievable. Her small apartment became cramped with ghosts from her past.

Henry and their promise of a life together—cut short by a car accident.

Her parents and their marriage. To Bridgette, the relationship had seemed so perfect as a child. Now it was fractured. Was the marriage broken beyond repair?

Then there was Luke and that long-forgotten memory. It had risen to the surface at the sight of him and left a stabbing pain in her chest.

The sound of a bubble bursting caught Bridgette's attention and drew her gaze into the kitchen.

Another bubble burst, splattering tomato soup atop the range.

"Damn." Rushing to the kitchen, she removed the pot from the stove. A grilled-cheese sandwich sizzled in a frying pan. She flipped it over, the cooked side dark but not burned. At least she hadn't ruined her dinner—or burned down the building.

After pouring the soup into a bowl, she set the sandwich on a plate. True, it wasn't the fine meal her mother would have prepared. Then again, it was *her* food prepared in *her* kitchen. Setting the steaming bowl on the table, Bridgette took a seat.

She'd seen her mother briefly, when she went to the house after work and picked up her bag. Her mother had been undeniably disappointed but loving all the same. It almost made it impossible to leave her parent's house—almost, but not completely.

Spooning a bite into her mouth, she shuddered.

The curtains were open still. The world outside the rain-streaked window was black as pitch.

Suddenly she felt exposed.

Wiping her mouth with a napkin, she rose from the table and crossed the room. Bridgette looked out of the window, her breath fogging on the glass.

There, on the deserted street, sodden with rain, was the same woman she'd noticed in the morning.

Bridgette recoiled, as if burned by the glass. True,

she hadn't lived in Braxville for years, yet some things were universal. A woman standing in a storm and constantly staring at a building wasn't normal.

What should she do? Call the police? Call her parents?

Pulling her curtains shut, Bridgette knew there was really only one person she should tell. It was Luke Walker.

She went across the hall and knocked on the door. It was answered almost immediately. Luke stood on the threshold. He'd stripped out of his flannel shirt and only wore a skintight T-shirt in faded green. Through the thin fabric, the muscles of his arms, chest and abs were unmistakable. His short hair was tousled, and for the span of a heartbeat Bridgette clearly remembered the feeling of his mouth on hers.

"Hey, what's up?" he asked.

For a moment, Bridgette couldn't recall what had been so important. "There's a woman standing in the rain and staring at the building. What's more, I saw her earlier today, parked on the street and watching this building. I'm no mental health expert, but behavior like that is odd."

Luke heaved a sigh. "You're right. It is odd."

A new idea settled on Bridgette, like snow on an undisturbed landscape. "You know the woman?"

"Her name is Julia Jones. We dated over the summer. It was only a few dates and I knew it wasn't going to work. I told her we were done. Apparently, she doesn't agree."

"She's your ex-girlfriend?"

"Hey, not all my exes are as beautiful, smart, talented and stable as you," he said.

Bridgette couldn't help but smile. "Gee, you know how to make a girl feel special and creep her out all at the same time."

Luke shrugged. The shirt rode up from his waistband, showing a sliver of rock-hard abs. "What can I say," he asked. "It's a gift."

"Shouldn't we call someone about your ex? She can't just keep staring at your building and… What does she want?"

"To be honest," said Luke. "I'm not sure. Trust me, I've talked to her more than once and tried to explain that she and I are no longer an item. Until now, I've blamed it all on her age. She's young—or youngish. Twenty-three years old."

"What about the police? There are laws against stalking, you know."

"I threatened to call the cops, but really I felt too much like a heel to file a complaint." Luke leaned on the doorjamb and crossed one foot over the other.

His legs were long and strong. Bridgette remembered the feeling of his thighs between hers and, despite herself, she blushed. "There has to be someone to contact and ask for help. Family? Friends?"

"Julia lives with her mother," said Luke. "Maybe now is the time to give her a call."

"Too bad Julia couldn't find someone else to like—someone who likes her in return."

"That's what I keep hoping will happen. That, or she'll get bored watching this place day after day."

The conversation reached a lull. Bridgette figured her soup was now cold and her sandwich had gotten soggy. "If you need me to do anything," Bridgette said. "Let me know. I'm happy to help."

"Sure," said Luke. "Hopefully, her mom will talk sense into Julia."

"Hopefully," said Bridgette. She gave Luke a little wave and returned to her apartment. She closed the door and pressed her forehead into the wood. Her heartbeat hammered against her ribs and her breath came in short gasps. It wasn't knowing about the slightly unhinged woman that left Bridgette agitated.

It was Luke.

Over the years, he had turned from a nice-looking boy into a handsome man. He was strong, smart, funny and caring. In short, Luke Walker was everything that Bridgette wanted in a man—that was if she wanted a man at all.

With him so near, she'd have to keep her emotions in check. It would be too easy to fall for Luke Walker a second time—and he was one mistake she refused to make twice.

Luke stared at the door to Bridgette's apartment long after it shut. She had been less than happy to see him at first, that was for sure. Had it been, as she claimed, shock that came out sideways and only appeared to be displeasure? Or had seeing him truly left her upset? For some reason, Luke would bet on the latter, although he didn't know why he'd place that wager.

Shaking his head, Luke stepped into his apartment and closed the door. At the window, he looked at the street below. There, soaking wet, was Julia. She stared up at his apartment. For a moment, their gazes met. She stepped forward, her hand outstretched.

He closed his curtains.

Bridgette was right. Julia staring at his apartment and store day after day was peculiar. Moreover, it was time her obsession ended. Lifting the phone from the charging stand, he used an app to find a number for Julia's mom. He'd only met Nancy Jones once. During that brief introduction, she appeared to be a caring woman, one who was truly concerned for her daughter's well-being.

He placed the call and it was answered on the second ring. "Yes?"

"Hi, Nancy. This is Luke Walker." He paused, not sure how to categorize his relationship with Julia.

Thankfully, Nancy saved him from thinking too hard. "Of course, I remember you, Luke. I'm sorry to say, but Julia is working late tonight."

"Working?" he echoed.

"Yes, she just called an hour ago and said that her boss needed her to stay late."

Luke pulled back the curtains and peeked through the seam between fabric and wall. Julia still stood on the street. Rain dripped from her dark hair and her clothes were soaked.

"Nancy, I hate to tell you this," said Luke. "But Julia isn't at work."

"No, you're mistaken. She called me."

"I'm not mistaken," said Luke. "Honestly, I wish I was. Julia has been watching my business and home for the past month and a half. She comes early in the morning and returns later in the day."

"Are you sure?"

"Positive," said Luke. "In fact, I'm looking at her right now. She's standing on Main Street and looking up at my apartment."

Nancy sucked in a breath. "I hoped that things had gotten better for Julia. That she was…well, better."

"Really, ma'am. I am so sorry. I didn't know what to do besides call you."

"No need to apologize," said Nancy. "You did the right thing. I'm going to call her now and see if I can talk her into coming home."

"Good luck," said Luke. Nancy had already ended the call and the line was dead.

Julia stood on the street, staring at the building and the closed curtains. Her phone, tucked into her jacket pocket, began to vibrate and trill. She glanced at the screen. It was her mother. Tucking the phone back into her pocket, she ignored the call.

She didn't have the time to be distracted.

Luke had made contact. The games they'd been playing were done and it was time to begin anew.

Rain fell in sheets. Julia's breath froze into a cloud before being washed away by the storm. Earlier, she'd started shivering. Now she couldn't feel her fingers or toes. Soon Luke would come to her. He'd bring her tea or maybe soup. He'd invite her to get warm and dry in his apartment.

It was almost like a scene in a movie—the same one the actor had been in.

Yet, this was not pretend. They were kindred spirits—soul mates, if you believed in that sort of thing. And, oh, Julia believed with every breath she drew and every beat of her racing heart.

Her phone shimmied again, shaking her jacket and sending a rivulet of rain streaming down her neck. It would be her mother again. Still, Julia couldn't leave. Not when Luke was coming down the stairs and would open the door right…now.

Or now.

Or now.

The door remained closed.

Maybe he was starting the kettle for tea. Or perhaps he was drawing a bath for them both. He'd be down any minute, like…now.

Her phone stopped ringing.

It began an instant later.

Julia fished the phone from her pocket and swiped the call open. "What, Mother? I am working."

"No," her mother said, her voice hoarse from crying. "You aren't. You're lying to me and—what's worse—lying to yourself."

Julia's face went numb. Her fingertips began to throb. How could her mother know? For months, Julia told her mother that she was employed as an administrative assistant at Colton Construction, working for Mr. Colton personally. The story was almost true. Julia did work at CC, just part-time and in the mail room. One day soon, though, she'd be noticed and promoted. "I'm in a meeting, Mother. I told you that already."

"You aren't working," said her mother, steel in her watery tone. "You are standing on the street in the pouring rain and staring at Luke Walker's apartment."

Julia's chest tightened, making it impossible to breathe. "Who told you such a lie?"

"Luke just called and said you've been stalking him."

"No," said Julia. "Luke will come to me any minute."

"He won't. Your relationship with that man is over. You need to get home now."

"I won't," said Julia, stomping her foot. She splashed a puddle, frigid water washing over her leg and shoe.

"Sweetie, you need to come home on your own right now, or I'm going to have to call the police. From there, you'll go to the hospital. You know that."

Not the hospital, with the piss-yellow floors and walls the color of a cloudy day. Not the hospital, where she had to take handfuls of pills that made Julia feel as if she was watching her pathetic life and not living it. Not the hospital, where the orderly told Julia she was pretty—beautiful, really—and left his hand on her thigh long enough for her skin to crawl.

She wasn't crazy. She didn't need to be locked up.

What she needed was Luke.

He was on his way—she could feel it in her bones. He was about to open the door…now.

Nothing.

"Julia," said her mother. "Answer me right this minute. If you don't, I'm hanging up and calling the police. Julia, are you there?"

"Yes, Momma. I'm here."

"Now, there's a good girl. You need to come home, you know that."

"Yes, Momma."

"Are you on your way?"

"Yes, Momma."

"And, Julia?"

"Yes, Momma."

"I do love you, honey. I only want what's best."

Julia ended the call and walked back to her car, her shoes squelching with each step. She started the engine, turning the heater to the highest setting. A blast of cold air shot from the vents.

Damn car.

The engine wouldn't be warm enough to make heat until she got home.

She sat behind the steering wheel, wet and trembling.

What had changed?

Had Luke really called her mother?

Did she dare to think—to hope—that her mother was lying?

Then again, if he had called, why?

And that brought her questions back, full circle.

What had changed?

Julia knew most every move Luke had made. Today was no different from any other. There were a few customers at the store early. She figured that had made him happy.

Why then was he angry at her?

If only they could talk.

That would have to wait for another day. If Julia

didn't get home soon, her mother would make good on her promise to call the police.

Julia recalled little of her drive, and soon she turned onto the quiet street where she lived with her mother. She pulled into the driveway as a thin tendril of heat leaked from the vent.

"Figures," Julia grumbled while putting the gear-shift into Park.

Her house sat at the back of a small yard. A single tree stood near the street. The branches were already bare and dripped rainwater onto the sidewalk. Twin lights in sconces on either side of the door were ablaze, washing the front stoop in a warm golden glow. She was home.

Yet, she knew her homecoming would be less welcoming than the front of the house.

Her mother would be furious at Julia for lying.

Too bad she couldn't sit in the car forever. Then again Julia was cold, wet and hungry. A little ire from her mother was a small price to pay for a warm house and a hot meal.

The storm had passed and a fine mist hung in the air. Shuffling from the car, Julia opened the front door. The air was warm and the savory scent of beef stew greeted her. Standing in the foyer, Julia slipped out of her coat and hung it on a stand. Rain dripped from the sleeves and gathered in a puddle on the floor.

The faint glow of the TV filled the darkened den. She didn't pause and try to find her mother in the gloom. Tiptoeing past the doorway, Julia hoped that tonight she'd get lucky. Maybe, she could get a bowl of stew from the kitchen and sneak into her room, never speaking once to her mother.

Stepping into the kitchen, Julia flipped a switch, filling the room with light. There, at the table, sat her mother. An oxygen tube ran from her nose to a small tank that was hooked to the back of the wheelchair.

It was years of smoking that had left her mother's body shriveled and racked with illnesses. The worst of it was that, despite her illness, Nancy's mind was fully intact. Years before, Julia's father had left to get cigarettes and never came back.

It was then that Julia's mother vowed to smoke forever. Though Julia never understood how that made her mother fearless or bold.

"Sit," said her mother, pointing to a seat opposite at the small table.

"I'm really wet and tired, Momma. I just want some stew. Can't I eat in my room, just this once?"

"You know I don't like food in the rooms—it brings about pests. I also don't like fibs. Lies. We need to talk."

Julia opened her mouth to argue but could think of nothing to say, and she dropped into the seat. Her mother wheeled herself to the stove. Slowly she lifted to standing. It took several minutes for Nancy to move along the kitchen counter, collecting a bowl, spoon and slices of bread.

Her stomach contracting painfully with hunger, Julia waited. Her mother liked to cook and prepare dinner. It gave her a sense of purpose, a glimpse into her former life.

Nancy placed the food in front of Julia with a *thunk* of crockery on faux wood. Brown broth sloshed over the bowl's lip, disappearing into the floral-patterned place mat. She set down sliced bread on a plate.

Dropping back into her chair, Nancy took deep gulps of air, as if she were drinking from a garden hose. It gave Julia a moment to eat before having to speak to her mother.

"Tell me the truth," said her mother after a moment. "What's going on."

Julia ripped a piece of bread and trailed it through the stew. "Nothing's going on."

"Let's start with the job. Is that made up? Do you work for Colton Construction—or anywhere at all?"

"I do work for Colton Construction," said Julia. "You've even seen my pay checks."

"But you aren't Mr. Colton's personal assistant, are you?"

Julia took a bite of bread. She swallowed, gagged and rushed to the sink for water.

"You aren't Mr. Colton's personal assistant, are you?" her mother asked. There was a sharp edge to her words.

Now, more than ever, Julia felt as if she walked on the razor's edge. She didn't know what to say. Leaning over the sink, her hair fell forward, a damp curtain shielding her from the rest of the world. She slurped from the faucet long after her thirst was sated.

Her mother asked, "What do you do at work?"

Wiping her mouth with the back of her hand, Julia said, "I'm in the mail room from ten o'clock in the morning until everything's delivered. Sometimes, I make copies or stuff envelopes. It's nothing glamorous."

"It's honest work. And you've been there since this summer?"

Julia nodded. "Yes, Momma."

"Sit down. Finish your stew and tell me about work."

Julia returned to the table and picked up her spoon. "I'm glad I can be honest with you, Momma. I wanted you to be proud of me, and assistant to the boss seems more important than sorting mail."

"I am so proud of you, Julia. Working and holding a job is hard—and look at you, honey. You've been employed for months." Her mother paused. "I wish you would have told me the truth from the beginning."

"I guess I should have," said Julia.

"We also need to talk about the boy."

"Boy?"

"Luke Walker."

"Momma, he's not a boy. He's a man."

"You can't hang around his apartment and store anymore."

"Listen, Momma," said Julia. "I just need to talk to him. If we speak, we can work out this misunderstanding."

Nancy placed her hand on Julia's wrist, the touch halting Julia's words. Her mother's fingers were gnarled, her skin thin and dry. "You have to let him go. Much as you like him, he has moved on. Do you hear me?"

"I hear you," said Julia. A sheen of grease floated on top of the stew and her stomach roiled.

"I'm glad we had this talk. Remember, you can tell me anything."

Julia stood and placed a kiss on her mother's cheek.

"I always remember." And then she said, "Do you want me to clean up the dishes?"

Nancy shook her head. "While I can still do a few things, I will. You go and put on something warm and dry. You must be cold—your lips are trembling."

Julia walked down the short hallway and slipped into her bedroom. She pressed the door closed with just the whisper of a sound. Her room was her sanctuary, a place her mother never entered. Standing in the dark, Julia stripped out of her damp clothes. With the cool air kissing her skin, she turned on the light. Every inch of her walls was covered.

There were photos of Luke Walker. Selfies of them both taken on each date—their smiling faces side by side forever. Then there were other pictures taken of Luke, those for which he hadn't posed. The one where he ran past Julia, shirtless and covered in sweat. There were several of Luke walking from the hardware store to the coffee shop, hands in pockets and gaze cast at the road. Or his return trip with a paper cup. There was one taken from across the street and through the front window of the hardware store. In that picture, Luke was nothing more than a shadow.

There was more than the pictures. Julia still had the stubs from the movie he took her to see. She had a napkin from the time they went to get ice cream and another from a roadside barbecue stand.

Tucked beneath her pillow and out of sight was a shirt Julia found draped over a ladder on the day that Luke cleaned the windows of Walker Hardware. She'd worn it to bed every night for months.

Much as her mother thought that Luke no longer cared, she was wrong.

Julia knew that she and Luke were meant to be together. Not just now, but always.

Chapter 5

Bridgette woke to sunlight streaming through sheer curtains. She stretched, taking up the whole bed. For the first time in years, she missed waking up in the arms of a man. She froze, mid-stretch. Breathless, she waited for the stab of guilt or the heaviness of grief to overtake her.

Neither came.

Was she ready to move on with her life even if it meant leaving memories of Henry behind?

More than that, was she ready to trust and hope and love for a second time?

Bridgette knew those kinds of thoughts were too deep to parse through without the benefit of coffee. Throwing back the blankets, she stood, stretched once more and padded to the kitchen. Last night, in her haste to move into her apartment, Bridgette had done only the most rudimentary shopping at the market. Cans of soup. Cheese. Bread. Cold cereal. Milk. Instant coffee.

Instant coffee and cold cereal seemed like a horrible way to start her day, especially since La Dolce Vita was right across the street. After pulling her hair into a ponytail and dressing in jeans and a sweatshirt, Bridgette pocketed her keys and credit card.

After taking the stairs to the ground floor, she stepped onto Main Street. Last night's rain was long gone, leaving behind a sky of robin's-egg blue, without a cloud in sight. The breeze still held a chill, and Bridgette was thankful for her sweatshirt. Jogging across the empty street, she pushed open the door to the coffee shop.

It was early, not yet six thirty, and still more than ten patrons filled the small shop. Megan Parker, the owner, looked up. "Morning, Bridgette," she said. Megan was nearly ten years older than Bridgette, and mother to several teenagers. A pleasant-looking woman with dark hair, Megan continued, "I'm glad to see you're back in town."

"Thanks," she said. "How's your husband and the kids?"

"The kids keep us busy, but my husband's been sick lately. Lots of doctor appointments while trying to figure out what's wrong. I'll tell you what, your dad's a saint. Chuck has been home more than on the job site and your father keeps paying our health insurance. Without Fitz, we'd be on the hook for everything."

Another employee of Colton Construction with a

mystery illness? It couldn't be a coincidence, could it? "Has your husband been tested for cancer?" Bridgette asked.

"Oh, yeah," said Megan. "Cancer. Thyroid. Liver failure. Heart disease. So far, nothing's been positive."

"You'll keep me posted?" Bridgette asked. It was more than being polite—his diagnosis could very well shape her investigation.

"Enough about me. How are you? Will you be in town long?"

"Only until my job is done," Bridgette said. "Then I go where the state of Kansas sends me."

"Must be nice to be around your folks. Your brothers and sisters."

Now that Bridgette had a place to call her own, she was able to honestly say, "It is nice to be back in Braxville. Nobody in Wichita has coffee as good as yours."

"Nobody?"

"Nope."

"That's quite the compliment. What can I get for you, then?" Megan asked.

Bridgette was about to order and then Luke came to mind. Certainly she owed him more of an apology for how she'd acted—or was that, overreacted—last night than a grumbled *sorry*.

"I'll take my usual and—" she paused "—what does Luke Walker typically order? I've rented an apartment in his building and want to drop off a little thank-you. He's being super flexible with my schedule."

"I know just what to fix," said Megan. "It won't take me a minute."

Bridgette moved to the end of the counter. A discarded newspaper from Wichita sat on an empty table. Picking up the paper, Bridgette scanned the headlines.

A set of bells chimed as the coffee shop's door opened. Her middle filled with a fluttering and she looked up from the paper. Immediately Bridgette knew that she was hoping to see Luke. And just as quickly she wondered why.

It wasn't him.

The person who walked through the door stole Bridgette's breath all the same.

It was the woman who'd been stalking Luke, his ex-girlfriend. Julia.

"Here you go," said Megan, holding two paper bags—one with Bridgette's croissant and the other with Luke's breakfast sandwich. There was also a drink tray with two cups. "Tell Luke I said hello."

Julia let out a hiss of surprise. Balling her hands into fists, she turned and glared. Anger radiated off her in a wave of heat.

Bridgette's instincts rose to the surface—fight or flight. With the bags in one hand and the tray in the other, she walked across the coffee shop. The slap of her soles on the tile floor kept time with her racing heart.

She reached for the door, her fingers brushing the cold brass handle. Then she paused. Hadn't Bridgette been stuck in the past, pining for a relationship that she'd never have? Moreover, she knew what it meant to be young and in love, possibly for the first time. Maybe this chance encounter was a way to help Julia get over Luke.

But how?

The answer came immediately. Hadn't Bridgette said that a new relationship always helped ease some of the pain of the old one? Actually, she had said that Julia needed to find a new man. What if Luke's ex believed that he'd found a new woman? Would that be enough?

Sipping her coffee, Bridgette turned. "You're Julia, right?"

"Yes."

"I thought so. Luke mentioned you last night."

"Me?" she squeaked. "What'd he say?"

"Just that you dated briefly, and things didn't work out."

Bridgette expected the other woman to look crestfallen—a necessary evil to get on with her life. She didn't. Her eyes flashed with an emotion so hard that Bridgette couldn't find a name.

"When did you speak to Luke?" Julia asked, her jaw clenched.

"Like I said, it was last night," Bridgette continued, knowing full well that she was alluding to time spent with Luke, which hadn't and wouldn't happen. She held up the twin bags of food. "I gotta go or breakfast will get cold." Bridgette stepped away.

"Hey," Julia called as Bridgette pushed the door open with her hip. "How well do you know Luke Walker?"

"In some ways, better than I know myself. We grew up together and were friends all the way through school. We dated toward the end of our senior year, but things unraveled when I went to college. I'm back for work." She shrugged. "We'll see how it goes."

Without another word, she opened the door and stepped into the bright morning. A line of cars passed, forcing Bridgette to wait at the curb. She glanced over her shoulder. There, at the coffee shop's window, stood Julia. The other woman splayed her palms against the glass. Her breath, collecting into a fog, obscured her face.

Despite the sun, Bridgette went cold.

With the traffic gone, she jogged across the street. At the door to the apartments, she worked the key into the lock. Every second seemed an eternity as Bridgette imagined the pain of a hand grabbing her from behind. The key slid home, turning the tumblers. She opened the door and stepped inside before kicking it shut with her heel.

For a moment, she stood in the silent foyer and listened to her racing heartbeat. Sweat dripped down her back and dotted her brow.

Without a doubt, Julia Jones was terrifying.

Moreover, Bridgette's chest was tight with worry. Had she taken a bad situation and made it worse?

Taking the staircase to the second floor, she paused briefly on the stoop before knocking on Luke's door.

Nothing.

She waited a minute and then a minute more.

Knocked. Waited.

Bridgette rapped her knuckles on the door for the third time. As she waited, she swore that she would knock no more. She didn't know Luke, at least not anymore. She didn't know his life or his schedule. He could exercise in the morning. Or already be at work. For all she knew, he actually had a girlfriend and never spent the night at his own place.

The bag in her hand became heavy. More than that, she felt ridiculous holding a tray with two cups when she'd obviously be eating breakfast alone.

She pivoted and strode to her own door.

"Hey, was that you?" Luke stood at his opened door. Speaking around a yawn, he continued. "I heard some knocking."

"I've woken you up. I am so sorry."

Luke's hair was tousled with sleep. His cheeks and chin were covered with the shadow of a beard. But what was worse—or maybe better—Luke wore only a pair of sleep pants that hung low on his hips. His pecs were covered with golden hair, before narrowing to a strip in the middle that dove straight down into the waistband. His abs were tight. His shoulders were broad and the muscles in his arms were well defined. He had the sexy V thing happening at his hips.

"I'm usually up at dawn for a run, but last night I had a hard time sleeping and skipped the workout." Rubbing sleep from his eyes, Luke asked, "What's the matter? Did something break?"

At least he'd been too tired to notice that Bridgette had been staring at—ogling, really—his bare chest.

"I brought over breakfast."

Luke blinked several times. "Breakfast?"

"You know, the first meal of the day. I also have coffee." She paused. "Besides, I owe you for how I acted last night. Really, it wasn't my best moment."

"I can't remember the last time anyone brought me a meal. That's really sweet of you."

"It's also really early and I've woken you up. I can just leave this for whenever you're ready."

Luke pulled the door open wider and stepped aside. "Don't be silly. Come in and eat with me. It gets old eating alone all the time."

Luke was right—solo meals were the worst. Bridgette stepped into Luke's apartment. It was the mirror image of her own yet with a lived-in feel. Several dirty dishes sat in the sink. Clean dishes stood in a strainer. A pile of old newspapers sat next to a rubbish bin. A thick binder was open on the coffee table.

"Have a seat," he said, and gestured to the sofa. "Let me put on something less comfortable. Then I'll get plates and mugs."

Luke disappeared into what she knew to be the bedroom. Sitting on the sofa, she peered at the binder. It was open to a page that listed vendors for the Braxville Boo-fest. Braxville Boo-fest? There was also an itinerary. Costume parade at 9:00 a.m. Hayrides from 10:00 a.m. until 4:00 p.m. Pumpkin lighting at 7:30 p.m. along with cider and doughnuts. Family-friendly haunted house during the hayride hours in the Ruby Row Center. Then there were plans for a scarier version that began after the pumpkin lighting.

Luke returned with both breakfasts plated, along with silverware rolled into a paper napkin. He'd changed, now wearing a pair of jeans and a faded T-shirt from KSU. Even with his chest covered, Luke was still undeniably fit.

"Here you go," he said, setting Bridgette's croissant in front of her. As he sat, his arm brushed her thigh. A shiver of something akin to anticipation traveled up her leg, taking root in the pit of her belly.

"Thanks," she said, taking a sip of her coffee. Pointing at the binder with her pinky, Bridgette asked, "What's this? I grew up in Braxville and have never heard of the Boo-fest."

"It's a new festival sponsored by the downtown businesses. This is only our fourth year. Basically, one Saturday in October we have a Halloween-themed fair. The stores decorate for the season. Kids and families can have fun and make a few nice memories. It brings people to the downtown who hopefully do a little shopping."

"Sounds like a great idea."

"It's a lot of work," said Luke before taking a bite of a breakfast sandwich. He chewed and swallowed. "I used to just be in charge of the parade. Line up judges for the costume contest. Get local businesses to donate prizes. You know the drill."

Bridgette didn't, yet she nodded in agreement.

"But then—" Luke took another bite and chewed slowly "—our chairperson up and quit yesterday, leaving me in charge of the whole event."

"Yikes."

"And I couldn't say no, even though I really feel like this is out of my league. And what's worse, there's less than two weeks for me to get up to speed and make it all happen."

Memories of Julia standing on the street corner and

in the rain came to mind. Was Luke such a nice guy that he'd never deny a request regardless of how difficult it was to fill? "Why can't you pass on the responsibility?" Bridgette asked.

"She has a medical emergency in the family."

"Oh. I guess you really can't turn her down, can you?"

Luke shook his head before sipping his coffee. "What I really need is someone to take over the parade. Doing two jobs while running the store is more work than even I can handle."

"I'm sure it'll be easy find someone willing to volunteer. Who wouldn't want to see all the adorable kids in costume? Oh, and you could do a pet costume parade, too."

"You could do it," said Luke.

"What? Me? No way. I'm busy. I have work."

"We all have work. But our job is to make Braxville a great community," he said. Nudging her with his shoulder, Luke winked and continued, "Besides, didn't you say you owe me?"

Certain he was teasing, Bridgette teased in return. "Owed. As in past tense. That's what your breakfast is for."

"Too bad," said Luke. "Your pet costume parade is a great idea."

Bridgette popped the last bite of croissant into her mouth before reaching for the binder. She scanned the duties for the parade chairperson. Organize a setup crew. Clean up. A big variety show was planned at the parade's conclusion in the mall. It looked like most of the plans had been made and volunteers already placed in time slots.

Maybe she could find an animal shelter to bring some pups to the parade. It would be a great way to help some dogs find their forever home. "I'm not saying that I'll chair the parade, Luke. But I can probably help out, at least a little."

"Really? I mean, thanks."

"Do you have one of these binders for the parade?"

"Me, put together a binder?" Luke snorted. "Not likely. I do have some papers with notes. How's this, we have a meeting tomorrow night at seven o'clock. It's at La Dolce Vita. Why don't you attend? You can get an idea of what's involved and then decide if you want to take on a leadership role."

Bridgette had come back to Braxville for work—not to get re-involved in life around town. Then again, even with all its imperfections, this place was her home. "Sure," she said, rising to her feet. "I'll check it out. Thanks."

She turned, reached for the door and pulled it open. Had less than a half hour passed since Bridgette had stood on the threshold, her heartbeat racing because of the encounter with Luke's ex-girlfriend.

Did the words exchanged with Julia warrant repeating?

She didn't think they did, especially if the other woman got the hint and left Luke alone.

"See you tomorrow night," she said. After giving a little wave, she stepped onto the landing.

"Hey, Bridgette."

She turned. Luke stood on the threshold.

"Yes?"

"You are full of surprises, you know. I'm glad that you came home even if you'll only be here for a little while."

Full of surprises. The phrase left her cold and light-headed. If Luke knew the secret that she'd kept all these years he might not think her so charming, and he definitely would not be happy to have her back in Braxville.

Julia's stomach roiled and felt as if she might retch. Gripping the mail cart's handle, she trudged down the hall. Each step was a struggle, as if she were wading through mud. Her thoughts were like a handful of pebbles in a stream, a jumble that tumbled over one another again and again.

Had Luke started dating someone else?

Had he really forgotten Julia?

Had the woman, Bridgette, really replaced Julia in Luke's life and in his heart?

And most important, how could she get him back?

A stack of letters lay atop the pile. All of them were addressed to Mr. Colton. As were her orders, Julia was to leave all correspondence with Mr. Colton's assistant. Today, her chair was empty.

The door to the boss's office was open. Sitting at his desk, head bent over a sheet of paper, Mr. Colton examined the report. Julia moved closer, as if drawn by a magnet. Was this her chance to meet the great man and perhaps impress him by showing diligence to her job.

She knocked softly. Mr. Colton looked up.

Julia held the stack of mail. "These are for you," she said. "Your assistant isn't at her desk and I wasn't sure…"

Before she finished her sentence, Mr. Colton dropped his eyes back to the report while holding out his hand. "I'll take them."

Stepping forward, she placed the mail in his outstretched palm. Her eye was drawn to a credenza at his back. The wooden top was filled with photos in expensive-looking frames of silver and gilt.

The largest one, set in the middle of the arrangement, was filled with smiling faces, all of them bearing a resemblance to each other and to Mr. Colton. Without question, it was a family photo. Right in the middle, smile wide and bright, with her arms wrapped around Mr. Colton's neck was Bridgette—the bitch.

Julia gasped.

Mr. Colton looked up from his desk. The overhead light reflected on the spot where his hair was thinning. "Can I help you with something else?"

Damn. She'd been caught staring. "That picture," said Julia. "The one with your wife and kids, I guess."

Mr. Colton spun around in his large leather chair. "This one?" he asked, picking up the frame before facing front.

"Yeah," she said. "I know that girl, the one in the middle."

"Bridgette? Did you go to school with her? Were you in her graduating class?"

If Bridgette and Luke were the same age, then they were both seven years older than Julia. She tried—

not successfully, though—to take no offense that Mr. Colton thought she looked to be over thirty years old.

"School? No, I think she's friends with my fricnd."

Mr. Colton set the picture on the corner of his desk. "Really? Who?"

"Luke Walker."

"Luke Walker. He was a good kid. Almost as smart as Bridgette. Damn shame his dad got ill. I always thought that Luke should've gone to engineering school. He was good with math, that one."

He was a good kid. Even though his daughter, an obvious slut, was spending the night at his apartment?

"It looks like you've got a lot of mail to deliver and I won't keep you," said Mr. Colton.

Julia knew when she'd been dismissed. "Have a nice day," she said, backing out of the office.

"Uh-huh," he said, not bothering to look up.

At first Julia thought she hated Bridgette for stealing Luke. But she had been wrong—she loathed the other woman. Bridgette's life was everything that Julia's should be.

Walking away, her thoughts focused to a razor-sharp edge. What Julia needed was a way to get rid of Bridgette Colton. But how?

Chapter 6

Bridgette spent her morning at the office and with the local staff. Going on much of the information provided by Ernest, her father's previous foreman, the team brainstormed possible causes of the cancer. The waters of nearby Lake Kanopolis. A naturally occurring carcinogen in the soil. Asbestos in the old elementary school. To Bridgette, none of the theories carried the ring of truth.

If it were something as common as lake water, the soil or the school, the number of illnesses would be at the level of an epidemic and not merely a cluster. Besides, each person in the case was male and of a similar age. There had to be something more that connected the men to one another.

Still, each theory needed to be examined and tested.

With the team gathered around the communal conference table, Bridgette ended the meeting by giving out assignments. "Adam, I want you and Carson to collect water and soil samples. Send them to the state lab and tell them we need the results stat."

"We're on it," said Adam.

With a nod, Bridgette continued, "Rachel, can you do some research on the old school? Are there other types of cancers that we're missing in the area, and if so, what are they?"

"What will you be up to, boss?" Carson asked.

"I'm going to look into the lives of each of the men on our list. My guess, there's something connecting them all. Something small. We just need to find that needle buried in the haystack."

After her coworkers left to do their respective jobs, Bridgette spent a few hours researching on the internet. There were eleven men in total, but she focused on three—Ernest O'Rourke, Bill Warner and Tom Cromwell.

Tom Cromwell had passed away long before the age of social media. Bill Warner had no presence on the internet, so there were no posts for her to stalk. Bridgette was able to access the archives for the Wichita paper, and there she found the obituary for each man. Bill Warner was divorced and survived by two children, who were both teenagers at the time of his death. She scribbled the names of the children on a piece of paper and made a note to look them up later. Tom Cromwell had been married when he passed away and had four children, ages ranging from five years old to preteens.

Bridgette wasn't sure how much the kids, who now were all adults, could add to her investigation. But if Tom's widow was still alive, she certainly could.

A quick internet search gave Bridgette the widow's name and phone number. Since the office phone showed up on any caller ID as the Kansas State Department of Health, Bridgette used an old handset and placed the call.

The call was answered on the second ring. "Hello?" a female asked. Her voice was thin, and Bridgette guessed she was speaking to Cromwell's widow.

"My name is Bridgette Colton, with the Kansas State Department of Health," she began, official as always. "Is this Mrs. Cromwell?"

"It is."

"I'm calling in regard to your late husband, Tom. I'm in Braxville, looking into a cluster of cancer cases. The name of your former husband has come up in our investigation."

"Cancer? That was years ago."

"I know it was, ma'am, but the state of Kansas has some follow-up questions."

"It's been two decades and now you care?"

Bridgette had expected some resistance, but what was she supposed to say to that? "Mrs. Cromwell, I work out of Wichita, but I grew up right here in Braxville. Something has made several of our community members sick and I'm determined to find out what it was." Or is.

"What'd you say your name was?"

"Bridgette. Bridgette Colton." Small towns being

what they are, she added, "I know your husband used to work for my father. I spoke with Ernest yesterday. He said that your late husband was one of his best friends."

"I suppose you could stop by," said Mrs. Cromwell, her reluctance beginning to wane.

"When?" asked Bridgette.

"I have an appointment at noon," the woman began.

Glancing over her shoulder, Bridgette looked at the wall clock. It was 9:45 a.m. "I can get to your house by quarter past ten," she said. "I swear to be gone by eleven thirty." In fact, the timing worked out perfectly for Bridgette. After all, she had promised to have lunch with her mother today.

"Well, I suppose that would be all right. Let me give you my address."

Despite the fact that Bridgette had used the state's database to find the woman, she waited patiently as the widow repeated the street name and house number. "I'll be by in a few minutes," said Bridgette, ending the call.

A cloudless Kansas sky stretched out before disappearing over the edges of an endless horizon. The Cromwell house was located on the edge of Braxville, where farmland and town meet. The home was a small square, with two windows on the second floor. The front door was in the middle of the ground level, along with a stoop, round and edged with brick.

As Bridgette pulled onto the gravel shoulder, she couldn't help but notice that the front of the house looked like a surprised face. As if the home itself was shocked by her arrival.

The door opened and a woman stood on the threshold. Until now, Bridgette had a mental image of an elderly woman with a home perm and a floral housecoat. Mrs. Cromwell was tall—nearly as tall as Bridgette—with jet-black hair. She wore a pair of jeans and a long-sleeved striped T-shirt. A golden cross hung from a chain around her neck.

"You must be Bridgette," she said, extending her palm to shake. "You look a good bit like your mother."

"I'll take that as a compliment, Mrs. Cromwell," said Bridgette, shaking the woman's hand.

"You should. Lilly is good people." Pivoting toward the door, she continued, "Come on in and call me Trish."

The front door led directly to a small living room. There was a floral sofa, coordinating recliner and a brick fireplace. A wooden coffee table sat in the middle of it all. A flat-screen TV hung above the empty hearth. Trish lowered herself onto one end of the sofa. Bridgette settled into the recliner.

A stack of papers and photo albums sat in the middle of the coffee table. Trish picked up the top item in the pile. It was a clipping from an old newspaper. She handed it to Bridgette. "That's my husband's obituary. He died almost eighteen years ago. Sometimes it seems like he's been gone a century. Other times," she said, and shrugged, "I forget that he won't be coming home."

Although Bridgette's job was to be investigate the cancer cases, not get involved with the subjects personally, her chest contracted as she listened to Trish speak. "I lost my husband, too," she said. "Car accident, two years ago. I can't count the number of times I've seen something that would make him laugh or heard something he'd find interesting. I'll pick up the phone to call. Then it hits me that he'll never answer, and it's like losing him all over again."

"I can't say those moments ever go away, but they don't happen as often." Trish reached for a photo album. Pressing the book to her chest, she stroked the cover. "Time never heals any wounds, but it does dull the pain."

"Thanks," said Bridgette. Her eyes stung and she blinked away the tears that were threatening to fall. "That means a lot to talk to someone who knows—really knows—what it's like."

"Look at us," said Trish. A single tear snaked down the side of her face. She wiped it away. "Spending the morning feeling sorry for ourselves. And you with a job to do. You said you wanted some information about my husband, so I dug all of this stuff out." She handed Bridgette the album. A date, twenty years prior, was written in faded marker on the cover. "Back then, I was into scrapbooking. I took pictures of everything, then glued them into these things with little stickers and such. Anyway, that book is from the year he got sick."

Bridgette flipped through the pages as Trish spoke. The first page was filled with pictures of a New Year's Eve party. She recognized Ernest's living room as not much had changed over the decades. In the middle of the page was a picture of Ernest, Tom and Bill. Arms were draped over one another's shoulders. The trio were glassy-eyed, and more than a dozen beer bottles sat on the table in front of them. A banner over the photo read: The Three Amigos.

But was there more? By summer, all of these men would be seriously sick. Was there a hint of the illness that was to come even as they rang in the New Year?

Bridgette flipped through a few more pages. Family photos, mostly. Snowball fights. A Valentine's party in an elementary school classroom. There was also a picture of Tom at work, his hair and face covered with plaster dust. He stood outside of one of the old Colton warehouses that became the downtown mall, Ruby Row Center. Bridgette remembered that project. It was the first big venture for Colton Construction. It launched the business from a small family-run company into the behemoth her father now ran.

The next picture was taken at the park near City Hall. Tom stood in front of a tree with branches covered in fluorescent green buds. It was obvious that he was ill. His face and arms were thin. His pallor was gray. His eyes were surrounded by dark circles.

"When was the first time you noticed your husband being sick?" Bridgette asked.

"He'd gotten what we thought was a cold around March. Aching. Sore throat. A cough that wouldn't go away. He started missing work. Ernest tried to cover for Tom, but in the end your dad had to let him go."

"I'm sorry," said Bridgett.

"Don't be. A man can't work, he can't expect to get paid. Anyway, your dad's a good boss and Tom was lucky enough to be able to keep his health insurance. We went to the doctor, who figured out it was cancer right away. He got treatment in Wichita and the cancer went into remission. Then it came back a few years later. Well, I guess it was then that Tom's luck had run out."

"Your husband and his two best friends ended up with a rare cancer at the same time. Did they have any theories as to what caused their illnesses?"

"They used to have a few jokes," said Trish. "Gallows humor, you'd call it."

"I know, Ernest told me. They thought that my dad was such a difficult boss that it gave them all cancer."

Trish gave a wry smile. "Ernest shouldn't have said that to you. It was bad of him to tease you about your dad."

"Don't worry," said Bridgette with a smile of her own. "I'm Fitz Colton's daughter. I understand that he's a hard man to please." She paused. "Back then, what did you think?"

"Honestly, I thought that they were so close—closer even than brothers—that one couldn't suffer without the others sharing the burden."

"That's very poignant," said Bridgette. Too bad it lacked a shred of scientific evidence. "Tell me about your husband's other jobs. Aside from Colton Construction when he got sick, where else did he work?"

Tom had a long list of jobs in manual labor. Most were in Kansas, but for a short while he had worked in Mississippi on an oil rig. The petroleum industry was notorious for using carcinogens in their processes, especially decades earlier, before awareness for worker safety had been raised.

While that might account for Tom developing cancer, it could hardly explain why anyone else had gotten sick. After spending an hour with Trish Cromwell, Bridgette had gotten a full history of the case. Still, she was no closer to solving the mystery of why so many in Braxville were stricken with cancer.

Bridgette pulled into the circular drive at her parents' home and parked the car. Sure, her mom and dad's constant arguing had spurred her to find her own place, but as she turned off the ignition she had to admit that it was nice to be home.

Bridgette was lost in thought. The reason for all the cancer cases was close, she could tell. But it was like looking for something she dropped in the grass on a foggy morning.

She opened the door without knocking and stepped inside. Even from the foyer, Bridgette could hear the raised voices of a man and woman in the midst of an argument. Was her father home? She hadn't seen his truck.

Setting her bag by the door, Bridgette walked toward the sound. They were coming from the kitchen.

"I just really wish you'd stop pressuring me about this, Shep," said her mother. "It's none of your concern."

Oh, so it was dad's half-brother, Shepherd, newly retired from the navy, with whom her mother was arguing. Then again, that brought up a whole new set of questions. What did Uncle Shep want her mother to do? And why was it none of his business?

She approached the kitchen and watched them from the doorway. Her mother had her back to the breakfast bar, her arms folded across her chest. Shep stood just feet away from Lilly. Hand lifted, he reached out to touch her mother. He hesitated, letting his palm linger above her shoulder.

"Hey, guys," said Bridgette a little brighter and louder than was necessary.

Her mother wiped her eyes quickly before turning. A smile lit up her face. "Oh, honey, you're home. I made us grilled chicken salads and, for dessert, apple tarts. I hope you're hungry."

"If I wasn't before," said Bridgette. "I would be now." She stepped into the kitchen and leaned into a hug from her uncle. "How's the guesthouse?" she asked.

"Nicer than a lot of other places I've lived."

"Shep just offered to move out and get an apartment in town so you could move back here," said Lilly as she arranged chicken and greens on two plates.

"You stay where you are," said Bridgette. Is that what had caused the quarrel? The fact that she'd moved from home when she would have stayed if the guesthouse were empty. Wanting to smooth any rough edges between her mother and uncle, she continued, "You're already settled. Besides, being in town and close to work makes my life easier."

"Thanks for understanding," said Shep. "I better get going, I told your dad I'd stop by the office."

He left the room. Lilly stared at the door even after Shep was gone. It left Bridgette searching for something to say. "Everything okay, Mom?" she asked after a moment.

"What?" Lilly asked. "Oh, of course. Everything's fine."

"You sure? You seem a little off."

"I've been a little tired lately. I might be coming down with a cold."

"Do you want to cancel the bonfire?"

"No, I'll feel worse if the whole family doesn't get together." Lilly patted the bar stool. "Have a seat. Can I get you tea? Coffee? A soda?"

"Just water," said Bridgette as she scooted onto the seat.

"Water it is," said Lilly, filling up two glasses with ice and filtered water from a dispenser in the fridge. "Here you go," she said, handing a glass to Bridgette.

As Bridgette took a sip, her mother slipped onto the bar stool to her left. Lifting a sheet of paper from the counter, Lilly said, "This is the quote I have from the caterer."

Bridgette scanned the list of food, drinks and desserts. Her mother certainly had ordered a nice meal for family and friends. Yet, Bridgette had inherited a good bit of her father's practicality and she choked a little as she looked at the total. "What if you changed the order to half ribs and half chicken, Mom? That way you give folks a variety and costs come down."

"I guess I could do that," said Lilly. "And maybe take away the green beans since I already have roasted squash and corn on the cob. Nobody expects too many vegetables at a barbecue, right?"

Scribbling numbers on the paper's margin, Bridgette added up the new total. "That's a number even Dad won't complain about," she said, setting the menu aside.

"Trust me," said Lilly with a wry laugh. "Your father can complain about anything."

"You know, Mom. I'm worried about you and Dad. You really don't seem to get along at all."

Lilly picked up her fork and pushed a piece of chicken across her plate. For a moment, Bridgette was left to wonder if her mother was going to say anything at all.

"I guess that's what happens to old married couples," she said at length. "It's funny, but for years I was the bookkeeper for Colton Construction. It was a struggle. I had all of you kids to look after. A house to keep and a husband who loved his work." She shook her head. "Those days, your dad and I would dream about having a big house and lots of money. Then it finally happened and look at us. We're closer to miserable now than when we had nothing." She dabbed at the corners of her eyes with a napkin and gave a wan smile. "I guess that's the definition of irony."

Reaching for her mother's hand, Bridgette said, "I'm sorry, Mom. Maybe you and Dad should take a vacation. You know, spend a little time together and reconnect."

"Maybe," said her mother in a way that made Bridgette think Lilly would do no such thing.

It seemed as if their conversation was at an end, and Bridgette hadn't even finished half of her salad. But her mother had mentioned something that piqued her interest personally and professionally.

She said, "I didn't know you used to help Dad with Colton Construction."

Lilly lifted one slender shoulder and let it drop. "It was cheaper for me to do the work than it was to pay someone else. In fact, I was basically the office manager. I sent out the invoices, paid outstanding debts and processed all the paychecks. I even did the taxes for the first few years."

"Do you have those old files?" Bridgette asked.

"Of course. You know how your father is about making sure we keep everything. Little good it would do. Technology is so much more advanced now. I don't know of any computer that can read a floppy disk nowadays."

Lilly's statement left Bridgette cold. Yesterday she'd asked her father for employee information. His answer was that he didn't have records from twenty years ago. Had her father lied? Or maybe he'd simply forgotten?

"Do you know where the disks are?"

"Sure do," she said. "Your father stored them in the crawl space of the guesthouse before Shep moved back."

"Can I have the disks?" Bridgette asked. "They might help me with something at work."

Lilly sat up straight. "Why would you want a bunch of old disks?"

Why? It was a reasonable question. First, she suspected that her father had lied about having access to old employee information. Which meant what? Bridgette didn't know, but she was determined to find out.

Chapter 7

Thursday morning, Luke began before dawn as always with his regular run. There was no note from Julia taped to the door. Nor was she or her car anywhere to be seen. Did he dare to hope that the call to her mother had solved all of his problems?

And if that was true, why in the hell had Luke waited so long?

The rest of the day unfolded. The store was filled with customers from open to close. Despite the constant activity, more than once he glanced at the clock, willing the day to end. Time passed slowly, minutes becoming hours.

As the sun dipped below the horizon, turning the sky orange and pink, he flicked off the lights and locked all the doors.

Finally, it was 7:00 p.m.

Time for the Braxville Boo-fest committee meeting. Moreover, it was another chance to see Bridgette Colton.

Carrying the binder given to him by Stacey under one arm, he strode across the street. As he crossed, Luke glanced up and down the road. He searched for Julia lurking in a doorway. Or her blue sedan parked at the curb and belching fumes.

She wasn't there.

As he pulled open the door to La Dolce Vita, all thoughts about his ex-girlfriend ended.

Standing at the counter was Bridgette Colton. The collar and cuffs of a white blouse were showing under a bright blue sweater. Her dark blond hair was pulled into a high ponytail and hung to the middle of her back. A pair of jeans hugged her hips and rear. She laughed, throwing back her head, and he got a glimpse of her throat.

For a moment, he had a clear vision of placing a kiss on Bridgette's neck.

Was it a memory from the summer they dated? Or was it a much more adult fantasy?

At the back of the room, several tables had been pushed together. Half a dozen people had already filled seats. Taking a to-go cup from the counter, Bridgette moved to the table and sat. A single chair remained at the head of the table.

Luke placed the binder on the table before sitting. He waited for a moment as the crowd got settled.

He began, "I'd like to thank everyone for coming.

However, I have some bad news. Stacey isn't able to chair the Boo-fest anymore. Her husband's having some health issues and needs her attention. I've agreed to be the festival chairperson and want to introduce Bridgette Colton. She's considering taking over my old position and being in charge of the parade. We spoke this morning and she has great ideas."

All eyes turned to Bridgette.

She waved the tips of her fingers. "First, I want to say that the parade looks like a lot of fun for families. I'd like to add something to the day. In Wichita, I volunteer at a local animal shelter. As you may guess, it's hard to find forever homes for pets in need. So, something like the Boo-fest and the parade are perfect ways to introduce homeless dogs to families. If chair, I'd work with a local shelter to make sure we get exposure for the animals."

"Great idea," said Megan Parker. "We adopted our dog, Skippy, a few years ago and he's definitely part of our family."

"I agree with Megan," said Luke. "It is a great idea. In fact, I'm a little jealous, Bridgette. You've had only a few hours to think about the parade and have come up with a fabulous idea. I had a whole year and never once thought to include a charity." Everyone chuckled. "Moving on, let's start with committee reports. Gladys, do you have anything new for the bake-off?"

An hour later, Luke was certain that all the correct permits had been filed with the city. Moreover, everyone knew their roles and all necessary plans were in place. "Today is Thursday. The festival is next Saturday.

That gives us a little more than a week between now and then. Trust me, we're all going to be busy," Luke continued. "But if we all chip in, we can make this a Braxville Boo-fest for the history books." There was one item that Stacey had yet to address. Luke hated to burden anyone further, yet it could make a difference for everyone in the downtown. "We need media coverage," he said. "I'm sure the local paper will cover the events, but that only comes out once a week. We need a connection to the Wichita market. Any suggestions?"

Luke looked around the table. Nobody met his gaze.

Bridgette lifted her hand. "I know a producer for one of the TV stations. She was my college roommate. I can't make any promises, but I can send her a message."

"That's great," said Luke. "Does this mean you're officially in charge of the parade?"

Bridgette already had her phone in her hand and was tapping on the screen. "I guess it does," she said as she sent the text. Her cell pinged immediately. "She says she's interested. I need to give her a press release. Do you have one?"

"No," said Megan. "We never tried to get any media coverage before."

"That's okay," said Bridgette. "I've done a few for work. Luke, if I can get some information from you, then I can put a release together."

The meeting was adjourned, but nobody left. Like always, Megan served coffee and cookies, giving everyone a chance to visit. Several people congratulated Luke on a job well-done. Yet, he wanted to talk to one person in particular—Bridgette.

The bake-off chairwoman, Gladys Soames, sat next to Bridgette at a table by the window. Carrying a plate of cookies, he approached as the elderly woman was saying, "Now, make sure to tell your mother about the bake-off. She makes the best apple tarts in the world and would win for sure."

Bridgette said, "When I see my mother next, I'll encourage her to enter the contest."

Gladys rose from her seat. "Thank you. You are certainly a dear."

Luke sat in the seat Gladys had vacated. He set down the plate and slid it toward Bridgette with the tip of his finger. She took a cookie and lifted it to her mouth. Before taking a bite, she said, "That went well. You're a natural leader."

He shrugged. "And you're a natural idea generator."

"I guess we make quite a team," said Bridgette with a smile.

"It's always been like that," he said.

Her smile faded and she looked out the window. Night had fallen, and the front window reflected the room—and Bridgette. An emotion filled her face, but in the glass he couldn't name what it was. Pain? Despair? Regret? Was she annoyed that he'd brought up their past?

All those years ago they'd been good together. Was that why he felt there was more to their relationship than a youthful folly.

She turned back to Luke. "When would you have time to work on a press release? I'm sure you have everything in that big binder of yours."

"I haven't looked through it all yet," he said. "I'm sure Stacey, that's the old chair, knows more than what's here, but I don't want to bother her, not with everything she's going through."

"What's going on?" Bridgette asked. She took a bite of cookie. A crumb clung to the corner of her mouth and she licked it away. How could she make eating a cookie look sexy?

"Stacey's husband has cancer," said Luke. "He had it a few years ago, but it seems as if it's come back."

"Cancer?" Bridgette's eyes went wide. "What kind?"

"I don't know what he has now, but a few years ago it was esophageal."

"Are you sure?"

"About Stacey's husband having had esophageal cancer? I'm positive."

Bridgette set her half-eaten cookie on a napkin and dusted her fingertips together. "What did Stacey's husband do for a living?"

"George is kind of a jack-of-all-trades. He does a little painting and home repairs. I think a lot of the older folks in town used him for maintenance—Gladys Soames, included."

Bridgette leaned forward and lowered her voice. "Do you know if Stacey's husband ever worked for Colton Construction?"

Answering her question with one of his own, he asked, "Did he work for your dad?"

"Yeah."

Luke knew that answer, as well. "He did, six or seven years ago, I think."

Bridgette stared, openmouthed, at Luke.

"Are you okay?" he asked.

No reply.

"Bridgette, are you feeling ill? What's the matter?"

Rising from her seat, she mumbled, "I have to go."

"What? Why? Is anything wrong?"

She shook her head but said nothing more. Without a backward glance, she left the coffee shop. Luke moved to the window and watched as she hustled across the street. She unlocked the door leading to the apartments, stepped inside and disappeared from sight.

Cell phone in hand, Bridgette took the stairs two at a time. She pulled up her contact list and placed a call before reaching the landing. Her heart hammered against her chest as the phone rang and rang and rang.

"This is Rachel. I can't take your call. Leave a message and I'll get back to you." *Beep.*

"Dammit," Bridgette cursed. She hung up and called again.

It was answered on the first ring.

"Bridgette, hi. Sorry I missed you. I was just washing up after dinner," said Rachel, the technical expert in her group.

"I have something for you and it's important."

"Sure. What can I do for you?"

Working the key into the lock with one hand, Bridgette held the phone with the other. She opened the door, stepped into her apartment and flipped on the light. There, in the middle of the coffee table, was the box provided by her mother. "I have some floppy disks that I need opened. Can you do that?"

There was a long pause. "Floppy disks?"

"Yeah. I have a theory about what might tie everyone in the cluster together, but it's all on disk."

"What kind?"

Bridgette read off the serial number.

"I have a friend who collects old computers. Let me talk to her and see if she has the right tech. If so, we'll be in business."

"And if not?"

"The disks can be opened. They just have to be sent to the state office. It'll take a while."

"What's a while? Days? Weeks?"

"Try months, like three or four."

"That's too long. See what your friend says and let me know."

Bridgette ended the call and dropped onto the sofa. She lifted a disk from the box and examined it from every angle. The little piece of plastic held the power to prove Bridgette's theory, and if her guess was right, then Colton Construction was at the center of the cancer cases.

For the first time in her life, she hoped that she was wrong.

Julia stood in a darkened doorway and watched. Her chest ached with longing and hatred. Had Luke Walker really replaced her with Bridgette Colton? What was it that Bridgette had that Julia didn't?

A fancy last name? A college degree? An important job?

Bridgette only had the luck of her birth. It's not hard to be successful when every opportunity has been given to you.

What Julia had was grit. Life hadn't been kind to her and yet she persevered.

Luke had to see that. Right?

Only moments before, Julia had watched as the other woman left the coffee shop and raced across the street, going through the door that led to the apartment building where Luke lived. A moment later, a curious thing happened. The lights had come on in the apartment across the hall from where Luke lived, the one that had been vacant for months. The shades were drawn, so Julia didn't know if Bridgette Colton had turned on the lights, but she felt safe in her presumption.

There was something else interesting about Bridgette. As she ran across the street, her shoulders had been hunched. Her complexion had gone pale. And Julia could have sworn that she'd seen tears in the other woman's eyes.

It brought up an interesting question. With a life as blessed as that of Bridgette Colton, what could possibly cause her any grief? Had she gotten into an argument with Luke?

This morning, Julia had assumed that Bridgette had spent the night with Luke and was possibly living with him now. But the lights in his apartment were dark. Was she only a neighbor?

Had picking up his breakfast been a polite gesture made by a woman brought up with impeccable manners?

Besides, that morning Mr. Colton had mentioned Bridgette being in Braxville temporarily for work. If her stay was short, why was she living downtown? Why not stay with her parents?

Julia had seen pictures on Google Earth. The Colton house was huge. It was the kind of place that Julia would kill to call home.

A minute later, Luke emerged from the coffee shop, as well. He carried a large binder and kept his head down while walking. There was a pull in her middle, like her soul was tethered to his, but Julia stepped back farther into the shadows.

He was the one who had called her mother and ruined everything.

What's worse? Julia knew that call had been placed at the behest of Bridgette Colton.

After looking both ways for traffic that never came downtown this late at night, Luke crossed the street. Breathless with anticipation, she watched and waited. A moment later, Luke's apartment erupted with lights. Julia laughed out loud.

He wasn't living with Bridgette, after all.

It meant that Julia still had a chance with Luke, so long as Bridgette wasn't a rival for Luke's affections.

That spoiled bitch needed to leave downtown Braxville not just for now, but for good. The sooner Julia could convince Bridgette to go back to her parents' house—more like mansion—the better it would be for everyone.

* * *

Dropping the binder onto the table, Luke flopped down on the sofa. As a small business owner, his work was never done, and that included making sure events like the Braxville Boo-fest were a success. He'd barely had time to look at more than a couple of pages, and if he was going to be the chairperson, then he was ultimately responsible for everything that happened.

More than that, his store needed attention. There were invoices to file, orders to place, shelves to stock.

Tonight, he lacked the motivation for them all.

And he knew the reason why.

It was Bridgette Colton. She'd been back in his life for less than forty-eight hours, and already she was under his skin. He itched with the need to see her, to speak to her, to touch her. More than once throughout the day she had come to mind. He read an article in an online paper and wondered about her opinion. A song on the radio brought back memories of the night they had spent at her family's cabin. The scent of coffee left him wondering if she'd make it a habit of stopping by his apartment every morning.

For the first time, his apartment felt too small. What was worse, Bridgette was too close. He grabbed his phone and walked back down the stairs to the street, placing a call as he went.

"Luke." The phone was answered after the fourth ring by his friend, Reese Carpenter. "What's up?"

"Got time for a beer?"

"With you? Absolutely. When and where?"

"How about now, at the pub near my place."

"Now? I thought you were like Cinderella and turned into a pumpkin after dark," said Reese. "You never go out because you have to be in the store at dawn."

"Are you going to bust my balls about working hard now?" Luke asked.

"You know I'd never give you a hard time for everything you do. You're my favorite workaholic."

"Maybe you should consider a career change to comedy," said Luke, returning the good-natured banter. He'd walked while speaking on the phone and was now at the pub. While pulling open the door, he said, "I'm here. I'll save you a seat."

The crowd for a Thursday night was light and only half of the tables were filled. Several TVs on the walls were tuned to a football game. He slid onto a bar stool and the bartender looked up. "What'll it be?"

Luke ordered a beer and an order of buffalo wings.

"Make that two," said Reese, taking a seat next to Luke.

"Thanks for meeting me, man," said Luke, offering his hand to shake.

"I figured this was either a celebration or a commiseration. Either way, I'm here. So, which is it?"

The bartender set two glasses with amber liquid at their elbows. Luke took a sip, letting the beer settle in his middle before answering. "I need some levelheaded advice. It's about a woman."

"The dark-haired girl from this summer?"

"No, I broke it off with her almost as quick as it began."

"Who then?"

What was Luke supposed to say about Bridgette? More than being Luke's friend, Reese was an officer with the Braxville police force and Jordana Colton's partner. Did he want to put his friend in a position where he had to keep a confidence. "I ran into an ex-girlfriend," he said.

"And how'd it go?"

"At first, she was really upset to see me. Then, this morning she stopped by with coffee to apologize. I saw her tonight and she was friendly until..." He paused. "Hell, I don't even know what happened. She said she had to go and ran out the door. It's like her mood changed—" he snapped his fingers "—like that."

"So she's mercurial?" Reese asked.

Luke took another swallow of beer. "You could say that."

"Was she that way when you dated her before?"

"No way, man. She was caring, smart, funny, beautiful, driven."

"And now?"

"She looks better now than she did when we dated, and that's saying a lot. She's still smart, driven and caring. It's just..." Luke stopped talking as the bartender set down plastic baskets filled with saucy and spicy wings. Plunging a wing into a side of ranch, he shook his head.

"It's just what?" Reese asked. "You don't know what you want?"

"Something like that," said Luke, taking a bite of his wing.

"And you haven't seen this woman for years, right?"

"A decade, at least."

"As far as I'm concerned," said Reese, "that makes the two of you strangers. You want my advice? Avoid your old love. No reason to make yourself crazy over someone who means nothing to you."

If Reese was right, that left Luke with only one thing to do. He had to avoid Bridgette Colton at all costs.

Chapter 8

Friday morning, Bridgette arrived before any of her coworkers. She'd brought the dusty old box of disks with her and it sat in the middle of the communal conference table. Heart thundering, she stared at it with as much dread as she might a bomb.

If her suspicion was right and the cancer cases were linked to her father's company, the news would be explosive.

The office door opened and Rachel, red-faced and sweating, stood pinned between the door and the jamb. She held a large box.

Bridgette rushed to her coworker's side. "Looks like you can use a little help," she said, propping the door with her foot and taking the box. Immediately, the weight of the box pulled Bridgette forward. “Jeez, this is heavy. What did you bring? Bricks?”

“This is one of the old computers I told you about. I thought it would be easier to bring it to work and see if we can get into the disks here than wait for me to take them to my friend.”

Bridgette set the box on the table with a *thunk*, her arms and back thankful that she’d set down the burden. Lifting one of the flaps, she peered inside. There was a tangle of wires alongside cubes of almond-colored plastic. “What is that?”

Rachel set a coil of wires on the table. “This is a computer circa 2005.”

“Technology certainly has come a long way,” said Bridgette. “What can I do to help?”

“You can start by telling me why we need this beast in the first place.”

Bridgette removed one of the disks and waved it as she spoke. Over the years, her mother had written on each of the labels with her neat handwriting. The ink, once black, had faded with the passage of time to gray. “I want to cross-reference the names of our cancer victims to the names on these.”

Taking the disk, Rachel read, “‘Employee Tax Information, Colton Construction.’” She paused. Lifting an eyebrow, she turned to Bridgette. “Colton Construction—as in your family’s business? What does this have to do with the cancer cases in Braxville?”

Bridgette hesitated. At the moment, all she had was a theory—less than a theory, really. It was more like a hunch. What if she was wrong, something she hoped with all her heart? Was she really willing to jeopardize her family's reputation on a guess?

Then again Bridgette was here to do a job. Besides, how could she ask her coworkers to trust her if she wasn't willing to trust them?

"On Tuesday I noticed that my father's old foreman, Ernest O'Rourke, was on the list of cases. I spoke to him and he mentioned that two of his buddies, both of whom had worked for Colton Construction, also developed esophageal cancer." She approached the whiteboard with all the names of the cancer victims. Using a dry-erase marker, Bridgette circled Ernest's name, along with his two compatriots. She continued, "Both of these men have since passed away. One died of cancer and the other had a heart attack."

"That's peculiar," said Rachel.

"Then last night," said Bridgette. "I learned that George Navolsky also worked for Colton Construction."

"We have a dozen men on the list and four of them used to work for Colton Construction," said Rachel, summing up the issue. "Thirty percent is a lot."

"Exactly," said Bridgette. "And these disks have information about the employees over the years. Once we access the data, we can cross-reference it with our list."

"I hate to ask, but how'd you get the disks?"

"My mother used to be the office manager," said Bridgette. "She kept everything organized by year. I asked for the disks and she gave them to me."

"I don't want to be overly nosy, but did you tell her why you needed employee data?"

Bridgette bristled at Rachel's cautious tone. "I said

it had something to do with work." Already she could feel her shoulders tightening with the need to defend her actions. "Since she didn't ask for any further explanation, I wasn't obliged to give her one. Besides, I spoke to my father about Ernest and his friends already. He's aware of the possible connection."

"It could also be said that since these people are your parents, you owed them complete transparency."

"Are you saying that I'm a bad daughter?"

"Of course not," said Rachel quickly. "But you know how these cases go. There can be lawsuits. Fines levied by the state."

Until now Bridgette had been concerned only about the impact the investigation would have on her relationship with her father. She could almost convince herself that if Colton Construction was somehow involved, he'd want to know. After all, there was nothing more important than the safety of his employees. Right?

True, it was naive not to worry about the optics of Bridgette Colton investigating Colton Construction. Who would believe that the inquiry had been fair and impartial?

It was then that Rachel voiced Bridgette's deepest fear. "Can you do it?" she asked. "Can you really investigate not just the company your father owns, but that defines your whole family, as well? Can you honestly be impartial?"

"I have a job," said Bridgette. "It's finding out what's causing all the cases of cancer in Braxville. I intend to conduct this study fully and professionally, following all leads." She gestured to the box of disks. "I brought those in, didn't I?"

Rachel shrugged. "I guess you did."

"If it will make you feel better," Bridgette continued, "I'll speak to both of my parents. I'll be seeing them later this evening."

"It's settled then," said Rachel, looking into the large box again. "I'll get this computer set up and we'll see if we can access the disks."

Bridgette moved to the whiteboard and studied the names of each of the men on the list. They were more than victims of their disease. They were fathers, brothers, husbands and friends. Countless lives had been altered by their illnesses. In the silence of her heart, Bridgette vowed to make things right for each of the men. Then again, what would she do if it meant putting herself at odds with the entire Colton clan?

Getting information from the old disks had proved harder than Bridgette hoped. By the end of the day, her team was no closer to reviewing the data. Late on Friday afternoon, she called the team together for a meeting to wrap up their progress for the first week.

"For now," said Rachel. "I'll continue to work on opening the disks. I have several more things I can try before I really am out of options."

"How long will that take?" Carson asked.

Picking up a pen, Rachel tapped the tabletop. "Two days," she said. "Maybe three."

"So, you keep working on your end until Wednesday. If we haven't made progress then the disks will be sent to the state office," said Bridgette.

"Sounds like a plan," said Rachel.

"Carson and I have taken samples and sent them to the state labs. We'll have results by the end of next week," said Adam.

"But we did a little investigating as well and found something interesting," Carson added.

"Do tell," said Bridgette.

Adam opened a file folder and spread out photocopies of old news articles. "It seems that twenty-two years ago, there was a massive flood in downtown Braxville. One of those once-in-five-hundred-years kind of flood."

Twenty-two years ago, Bridgette would have been in elementary school—probably second grade. She lived outside of town. Yet, she had a vague memory of school being canceled for several days because of a flood. Was it the same one? It seemed as if it had been. "Go on," she urged.

"The entire town was affected, including an old petroleum station that was never reopened. The cleanup effort was massive. From reading these old articles, it seems like the townsfolk pitched in." He pointed to the whiteboard. "It's our theory that those on the list all helped."

"So, what's your conjecture?" Bridgette asked.

"Carcinogens were released in the floodwater," said Adam. "And then people were exposed during remediation."

"There's a problem with your theory," said Bridgette. "Lots of people helped rebuild downtown Braxville, correct?"

"There were truly hundreds involved," said Carson.

"Then, why aren't they sick, as well?"

"A combination of factors—gender, age, working after the flood—that came together to make a perfect storm," suggested Rachel.

"Or," said Carson, "maybe they all worked on removing debris from the same building. Could be something in the materials. Safety back when Braxville was founded isn't the same as it is today."

"Or maybe they didn't wear the proper gear for the type of cleanup they were doing," said Rachel.

Bridgette nodded. "I think you have found a trail worth following. Keep it up and let's see where it leads. We've only been on the case for a week, and a shortened one at that. A lot of progress has been made. Good job, everyone."

"Thanks, boss," said Adam.

"Then if there's nothing else to discuss," said Bridgette. "I want you all to have a great weekend and I'll see you on Monday."

Bridgette's coworkers packed up tote bags and briefcases before saying goodbye. Bridgette remained at her spot.

Carson stood at the door. "Aren't you going home, too?" he asked.

"I'm going to reread these articles you found. I grew up right here in Braxville but don't remember anything about a big flood."

"How old would you have been two decades ago?" he asked. "You were a kid. Unless your house was flooded, you might have no memory."

What Carson said was true. Then again… "I feel like

there was a lot I overlooked as a kid and am trying to find all the missing pieces."

"I'm going," said Carson, gesturing to the hallway with his chin. "As long as you promise to follow your own orders."

"Oh, yeah? What are those?"

"To enjoy your weekend."

"I will," said Bridgette. "I promise."

"Why do I feel as if you're planning on working every day?"

"My parents have a bonfire and barbecue every year in the fall. Mom sets tables out on the yard, right near the lake. Then we have too much food and too many drinks. Tonight's the night, so I can't stay too long at work even if I wanted."

"All right then," said Carson. "See you Monday."

Then it was Bridgette alone. She read all of the news coverage about the flood and the effort to rebuild and revitalize Braxville. To her, it seemed to be precursor to the Keep Braxville Beautiful initiative. Her father was mentioned in more than one of the articles. And in the quiet office—in the silence of her heart—Bridgette was more than a little relieved to have a lead that wasn't connected to Colton Construction.

Her phone pinged with an incoming text from Yvette. Are you almost here?

Bridgette glanced at the time. It was 6:30 p.m.

Damn. She was running late.

Tapping out a reply, she rose from her seat. On my way.

After rushing from her office, she made her way down Main Street. As she walked, Bridgette couldn't help but imagine what downtown Braxville must have looked like during the flood. With water chest high, every building would have been submerged. She could well imagine the toxins that ended up in the waters.

Was the flood to blame? Were the men who got sick sadly victims of being good citizens? Was it really what her father had said from the beginning—just bad luck?

The sun had dipped below the horizon, leaving the downtown in shadows. A breeze blew down the sidewalk, carrying a chill and the scent of rain. The door to her apartment was just ahead, but as she walked closer, Bridgette decided not to stop. She was late enough already and didn't have time to waste with changing out of her work attire.

Her car was directly in front of the hardware store. The convenient parking spot was a perk of renting the apartment from Luke. She cast a glance at the store as she passed. The lights were off, but that didn't stop her from searching the dim interior.

He wasn't there.

It was then that she caught sight of something in her periphery. The handle of a broken kitchen knife lay in the gutter. She knew what it meant before seeing anything further. Her tire had been slashed.

Bridgette rounded her car, her anger a hot flame that burst into an inferno. It wasn't just a single tire that had been cut. All four of them were completely flat. Replacing one flat tire with a spare was an inconvenience. Finding replacements for all four wheels, especially after six o'clock on a Friday night was damn near to impossible.

* * *

Like he did every Friday, Luke closed the store at five thirty. It didn't mean his work was done, or even close. Preparing for the busy weekend, he always spent the evening stocking the shelves.

"One hour in," he said, glancing at the clock on the stockroom wall. "I'm almost halfway done."

Sure, there was nobody to hear him speak.

And true, stocking shelves was a lame way to begin his weekend, especially since he was thirty-one years old and single.

Grabbing a box of washers from the shelf, Luke walked back to the store. His eye was drawn to the window and the street beyond. Even with her back to him, he recognized Bridgette Colton. Her dark blond hair. Her long legs and shapely rear. He couldn't look away even if he wanted. Then again, there was more to see than her nicely shaped female form. All four tires of her car were flat—an unlikely accident.

For Luke, it was impossible to ignore someone in need. Setting the box on the counter, he opened the door and stepped onto the sidewalk. "Need some help, Bridgette?" he asked.

"All of my tires have been slashed," she said, gesturing to her car. "I guess some kids thinking they're being funny."

"I can fix one tire," said Luke with a shake of his head. "But not all four. You'll have to get it towed in the morning. The garage should get it back on the road in a few hours."

"Tomorrow? A few hours?" Leaning on her car, she sighed heavily.

Luke told himself that he didn't care. He'd sworn not to get involved with the complicated Bridgette Colton. He knew all of that to be true, so why then did he ask. "Did you need to get somewhere? I can drop you off, if you'd like."

Bridgette waved away his offer to help. "It's at my parents' house. I can't ask you to take me. You'd waste an hour with the round trip. I can't ask you to ruin your Friday night on my account."

"Would it matter at all if I said you aren't ruining anything? I didn't have any plans, so this will at least get me out of the apartment."

"You're kidding?" She turned to face him. "A good-looking guy like you without a date on Friday night? I find that incredibly suspicious, Luke Walker."

Good-looking guy? Was she flirting with him? To be honest, he wouldn't mind if she was so long as he remembered that her moods were as changeable as the Kansas weather. "Honestly," he said with a laugh. "I haven't had a date in months."

"Months? What do you do to keep yourself busy?" Bridgette held up her hands. "Forget I asked. My sisters, especially Jordana, are always pushing me to date more, get out more, get over...well, the past more. I understand that she cares, but at times it can be a touch intrusive."

"Is that sort of like all the well-meaning customers who want to know if I'm dating anyone. Or when I plan to get married. Or if I want to get married at all."

"Ugh." Bridgette made a sour face. "You, too?"

"Still," he said, "I can give you a ride to your parents' house. It's not a problem."

"Sure," she said. "So long as you do me one favor."

"Anything," he said.

"Stay at the bonfire. There will be lots of food. Barbecued ribs and chicken. My parents will be happy to see you. All my siblings will be there. You can catch up with Brooks and Neil."

"Really," said Luke. "I shouldn't." He hooked his thumb toward the hardware store. "I've got lots to keep me busy."

"I mean, sure. I get it. You have responsibilities. But, really, I won't make you drive me all the way to my folks if you aren't staying. Maybe someone else is running late and can give me a ride. I'll send a text or something."

Had Luke just turned down an invitation to go to the bonfire? Hadn't he just been feeling sorry for himself and his lack of a social life? Had he said no just to avoid spending time with Bridgette, someone he wanted to be around a lot more?

Then there was her mention of the past. Of course, he'd heard how her husband died in a car accident. Even as kids, Bridgette had never been one to share her feelings. Perhaps the fact that she was friendly or not had more to do with being a young widow than anything else.

"On second thought," said Luke. "If the offer for the party still stands, I'd love to stay."

Phone in hand, Bridgette was typing out a message. "Are you sure? I mean, I'd love for you to come and would really appreciate the ride."

"Give me one minute to lock up the store and we can get going."

"Speaking of the store." Bridgette followed Luke to the front door. "Do you have any security cameras that might have caught whoever slashed my tires? Something I could turn over to the police?"

"Braxville is still a pretty safe community, so I've never needed the extra security of cameras," he said. Then again, he didn't think that local kids were involved. In fact, Luke was almost positive that he knew what happened to Bridgette's car.

The question was why would she be a target?

Sitting in the front seat of her car, Julia watched the scene unfold. As Luke held the door to his pickup truck open for Bridgette and she slipped into the passenger seat, Julia's chin began to quiver. It was unbelievable that her plan had utterly failed.

Luke rounded to the driver's side. He started the engine and the truck pulled away from the curb. Slamming her hand on the steering wheel, Julia said, "No. No. No."

Bridgette was supposed to be upset by the damage done to her car.

Luke wasn't supposed to care.

And they sure as hell weren't supposed to leave together.

Julia slumped lower in her seat as they drove past the corner where she'd parked. Turning her gaze to the side-view mirror, she watched until their taillights were little more than angry red eyes piercing the gathering darkness.

Starting the ignition, she hesitated only a moment

before pulling onto the street and rounding the corner. Luke's truck was more than a quarter of a mile ahead of Julia's car, but he was easy to follow.

They left Braxville, passing farmland and open fields. He turned toward the newly developed area where the houses were newer, larger, with long and winding driveways in front and pools in the back.

Even without a map, she knew where they were going. To Bridgette Colton's house.

As she drove, Julia's phone began to ring. A bracket held the cell in an air vent. Her mother's image and number appeared on the screen. Dammit.

She swiped the call open. "What do you need, Mother?"

"When are you coming home?" her mother asked, her voice all but drowned out by the road noise and the engine's whine.

"I'm going to a friend's house," Julia said. "One of the girls from work, Bridgette, invited me over for dinner."

"Are you sure?"

Julia ground her teeth together. True, she was telling her mother a lie, but what cause did her mom have to question where she was going or what she was doing? "I'm positive," she said, her teeth still gritted.

"Where does she live?"

Julia repeated the Coltons' address for her mother. She'd memorized it from all the times she looked at the house on the internet.

"All right," said her mom. "Well, I hope you have a nice time."

"I will," she said, as Luke pulled into the driveway of the Coltons' large and modern house.

The Colton home was in a private community, one that Julia couldn't enter. Eyes trained on the road, she passed the large gates and guard shack. She turned onto a frontage road and found a spot behind a large tree that gave her a perfect view of the Colton house.

She'd stowed a set of binoculars that had belonged to her father in the glove box. After removing them, Julia looked through the ocular lens, and the home came into view. With lights illuminating on the brick-and-wood facade, the home was more breathtaking in person than it had been in the pictures on the internet.

Holding her breath, Julia knew better than to hope. Could it be that Luke was only bringing Bridgett home? Was he simply a ride, a glorified taxi?

At almost the same instant, both doors opened. They jumped from the truck and Bridgette pointed to the side of the house. In the distance, sparks from a bonfire rose into the night.

Luke and Bridgette walked side by side. From her vantage point in the car, Julia was able to observe them, seeing things that she doubted they even saw. Luke stole glimpses of Bridgette, and she of him. She noted even more than their sly observations. Both Bridgette and Luke regarded each other with affection, attraction...love.

Julia refused to lose Luke.

Still, it brought up interesting and important questions. How far was Julia willing to go to keep Luke? What was she willing to do?

Chapter 9

Bridgette led Luke to the backyard. Side by side, they were so close that their hands brushed as they walked. His skin was warm. A tingling began in her fingers and traveled all the way up her arm, until her heart began to race. Folding her arms across her chest, she vowed to forget all about the sensation.

The scent of woodsmoke, along with the sounds of voices and laughter, filled the evening air. Her family was gathered at the back of the house. A long table with a white tablecloth was filled with food. Closer to the water's edge were several round tables, already filled with family, friends and neighbors. Candles of different heights and colors flickered on every surface. At the edge of the lawn was a community lake. The bonfire burned near the water, sending sparks into the sky, where they mingled with the stars before burning out.

Her mother, dressed in slim jeans, a turtleneck sweater and barn jacket, looked up as Bridgette approached. "There you are, honey," she said. "I was starting to get concerned."

Leaning in to kiss her mother's cheek, she said, "I had car trouble." Sure, her excuse wasn't the whole truth, but she didn't want her mother to worry or insist that Bridgette move back into the house. "You remember Luke Walker? He gave me a ride."

Luke stepped forward with his palm outstretched. "Pleasure to see you again, Mrs. Colton."

"You can call me Lilly," she said, pulling Luke into an embrace. "And here, we hug."

"You can count me out on that one." Bridgette didn't need to turn around. It was one of her triplet brothers, Brooks. Brooks and Luke had played baseball together in high school. "But it is good to see you, Luke."

"Good to see you, too," said Luke, as the two men shook hands and exchanged slaps on the back.

Brooks gave Bridgette a kiss on the cheek. "Good to see you, sis."

"You, too. You look good. How's work?"

"I'm still trying to figure out how two bodies ended up buried in the wall in a building in downtown Braxville."

"Aren't the police involved?" Bridgette asked.

"They are, but I've been hired to figure out what happened. How about you?" he asked. "What brings you to Braxville?"

"Work," she said, giving away nothing. Sure, she was being cagey. And true, Brooks might have heard rumors about the cancer cases and connected her to the investigation. All the same, Bridgette lived by a simple rule to never mix work and family.

"Obviously, it's work. You're also avoiding my question," Brooks continued with a smile. "Or is it a big secret?"

Sure, her brother was teasing. All the same, he was closer to the truth than anyone would have ever guessed.

Bridgette was saved from answering any more questions when the other triplet, Neil, along with the eldest Colton sibling, Tyler, called out, "Walker? Is that you?" He ambled over from the bonfire to greet Luke.

Her older sister, Jordana, approached. She wore a red sweater and jeans. Her sister's casual look left Bridgette wishing that she had taken time to change out of her slacks, blouse and blazer. Next to Jordana was a man, with dark hair and dark eyes.

Since she'd never met the man, she guessed that the guy was Jordana's new love, Clint.

"Looks to me like Luke's popular," Jordana said, hitching her chin toward the knot of men, all now with beers in hand, talking and laughing. "Our brothers wouldn't be more excited if you'd brought a puppy to the party."

"Luke's a good guy, that's for sure. Without him, I wouldn't have made it here at all."

"Bridgette, I want to introduce you to Clint," said Jordana. "This my sister Bridgette."

"It's great to meet you," Bridgette said. "You've made my sister very happy."

"Your sister is the one who's made me happy. More than that, your family is one of the nicest I've met. And Braxville is a special little town."

The mention of Braxville brought Bridgette's thoughts around to her car and the flat tires. "Jordana, you're a cop."

Her sister laughed. "Last time I checked, at least."

"Have you heard anything about kids slashing tires downtown?"

"Not a thing," Jordana said with the shake of her head. "Is that what's wrong with your car? Someone cut your tire?"

"Try tires. All four of them were completely flat."

"We haven't gotten any complaints, but I'll ask around and let you know if I hear anything." Tilting her head toward the house, Jordana said, "You want to come with me and help Mom inside? It looks like Brooks's newest girlfriend is inside, too."

"Brooks brought his girlfriend?" Bridgette asked, happy that her brother had finally found love. "I have to meet her." As they walked toward the house, their father's business partner, Uncle Dex, arrived with his wife, Mary.

"Bridgette, Jordana. Good to see you both. Where are you off to?"

"Helping Mom," said Jordana.

At the same moment, Bridgette said, "Going to meet Brooks's new lady friend."

Dex lifted his eyebrows. "About time Brooks found someone special. What'd you say her name was?"

Jordana answered the question. "Gwen," she said. "Gwen Harrison."

Dex went pale.

His wife gripped his arm. "Are you okay, Markus? You look like someone just walked on your grave."

"Just a little light-headed, that's all. Maybe I should grab a bite to eat. I'm sure that'll help me feel better."

Bridgette watched Dex approach the group of men and accept an offered beer. He most certainly didn't look piqued anymore. Was it her imagination or had Dex reacted badly to the mention of Brooks's new girlfriend?

Then again, she had more pressing concerns than anyone's opinion of her brother's latest love interest. Like, what had actually happened to her car?

Was there really a connection between the cancer cases and Colton Construction?

And, finally, how could she tell her parents—her father, especially—that their business might play a prominent role in her investigation?

After a few paces, Jordana stopped and turned to Bridgette. "Are you coming?" she asked. "Or what?"

"On my way," she said, jogging to catch up to her sister. To Bridgette, it seemed like everyone in Braxville had a secret. Walking into the bright and warm kitchen, she wondered how far people would go to keep those secrets hidden?

In all honesty, Luke enjoyed spending time with the Colton clan. It was a large and loud family, and completely different from what he had grown up with—just his parents and himself.

"Remember that time," said Ty. "I think you guys were all seniors in high school and it was the quarter-final game for state baseball championship."

Luke groaned. "Don't remind me, please."

They were all laughing at the memory. Ty continued, "You two were in the outfield." He slapped both Luke and Brooks on the back. "The batter hit the ball. It was headed for the fence. You both were looking at the ball—not each other. Then, smack, you ran into each other, knocking yourselves over."

Brooks and Neil roared with laughter at Ty's retelling of the tale. Luke couldn't help himself. With a shake of his head, he joined in the laughter.

"There you two were, lying on the field. For all we knew, you'd knocked each other out cold. Then Luke lifts his hand, straight in the air. Plop. The ball lands in his glove. The batter is out. The inning was over."

"Too bad we were down by four runs and never had a chance to make them up," said Luke.

As kids, Luke was always friends with the Colton boys. As men, they were people to be admired and respected. Why then, did he keep glancing over his shoulder, looking for Bridgette? More than that, where had she gone?

"To this day, that play is the best—and worst—I have ever seen in my life," Ty concluded, wiping his eyes with the back of his hand.

"Hey," said Neil. "I heard a rumor that you're now

in charge of the Braxville Boo-fest, Luke. How's that going?"

"Thankfully, the former chair had a good bit of planning done. Since it's next weekend, I'll have a busy few days, that's for sure. Still, if everyone pitches in it'll be a success."

"I'm glad to see that the downtown businesses are coming together," said Ty. "It creates a sense of community."

"That's what we're all hoping," said Luke, before finishing the last swallow of his beer.

"You need another drink?" Neil asked. "I'll get you one. The cooler's empty so I'll have to grab you one from inside."

Luke's gaze traveled to the house. Through a kitchen window, he spied Bridgette. She was smiling and shaking her head. She looked over her shoulder, said something and laughed. What Luke remembered best about the quarterfinal baseball game was that his single well-timed catch had given him enough confidence to ask Bridgette to prom.

She'd been at the game. All the Coltons had come to watch Brooks. Walking through the parking lot, Bridgette had lagged behind the rest of her family. Luke had left his parents and jogged to her side.

"Bridgette. Wait up," he had said.

Even now he recalled how his heart had thundered against his chest. It was the same feeling he had every time he saw her—anticipation, excitement, along with the promise of something better.

"Sorry about the game," she said. "You played really well."

His mouth went dry. His palms were damp. "So, now that baseball season is over, I guess we have to move on to what's next."

"Like finals. Graduation. College."

"I was thinking about prom."

She had shrugged and looked over her shoulder. Facing him again, she said, "I'm not going."

Luke's heart dropped to his shoes. "Why not?"

"First, nobody has asked."

Before losing his nerve, he said, "Want to go with me? I mean, I can take you. I mean, I'd love it if you wanted to go with me, too."

Crossing her arms over her chest, Bridgette had planted her feet on the ground. "Did my brother put you up to this?"

"Who? Brooks? No, never."

Eyes narrowed, she asked, "Why are you asking me?"

Luke had been deaf to every sound other than the pulse that roared in his ears. "Because I like you. You're cool."

She'd smiled and Luke no longer cared about the baseball game. Making Bridgette happy—that's what mattered. She dragged her toe through the gravel and nodded.

"Is that a yes?" he asked.

"Yeah," she had said. "I guess it is."

"Hey, Luke," Neil asked again, bringing him back to the present. "You need another beer?"

Bridgette still stood beside the window. He felt a pull like a magnet to steel, but a thousand times stronger. "I'll go grab them. Four?"

All the Colton brothers nodded, and Luke walked across the darkened lawn toward the house. He opened the door just as Lilly Colton arrived with a tray of steaming and saucy ribs. He held the door as she passed. "Thank you, Luke."

Yet, Lilly was just the first in a long parade of those carrying food. Jordana had grilled chicken, Yvette, a large salad, and an auburn-haired woman—who he guessed was Brooks's new girlfriend—held a large tray of corn.

As the women walked through the gathering darkness, Lilly looked over her shoulder. "Dinner's being served, Luke. See if you can't get Bridgette out of the house so we can eat."

"I'll do my best," said Luke before slipping inside. The door to the patio led to a large dining room, complete with a brass-and-crystal chandelier. Through a narrow archway was the adjoining kitchen.

Just like he'd seen from outside, Bridgette stood at the sink. She looked up as he entered. Her arms were in soapy water up to her elbows. "The caterer didn't send flatware for serving, so I'm washing some of Mom's."

"Do you need help? I'm pretty handy with soap and a sponge." Good Lord, had he really just said that? It was undoubtedly the cheesiest line known to man.

Bridgette tilted her head toward a dripping pile of silverware lying on a towel. "You can dry those off," she said.

He reached for another dish towel at the same moment that Bridgette yelped and drew her arm from the water. She cradled it to her chest.

"What happened?" he asked. He reached for her injured hand and wrapped it in the towel, squeezing enough to apply pressure.

"I nicked myself on the tines of a fork, I think," she said.

Luke removed the towel and wiped away the blood. A small gash on the side of her pinky finger wept blood. Bridgette's breath washed over his shoulder. The heat from her body warmed his skin. To see her wounded filled him with a desire to make her better and always keep her safe.

He ignored it all, and said, "Looks like you did get cut. Do you have any antibiotic ointment and a bandage?"

She pointed to a cabinet with her free hand. "In there."

A first-aid kit sat on the second shelf. As he rummaged through the contents, Luke tried not to think about how much he liked holding Bridgette's hand. Or how having her close brought back memories of a time when he was younger and anything was possible.

With bandage and ointment in hand, he turned back to Bridgette. "Got it," he said.

"Thanks." Bridgette took a moment to wash and dry her injury. Then she reached for the tube of ointment and applied a dab. After opening the bandage, Bridgette tried to center the adhesive tabs on the side of her hand.

"Do you mind?" she asked. "Getting this bandage on is awkward."

"Not at all," said Luke, a little too fast to be anything other than eager to touch her again. "I'm happy to help if you need it."

"Thanks," she said.

Luke smoothed the bandage over the cut. "There," he said. "Good as new." Yet, her hand remained in his. She didn't pull away. Luke dared to look at Bridgette. She was watching him. Their gazes met and held. He moved closer to her, so close that he could smell the lightly floral scent of her shampoo.

She inched forward, closing the distance between them. He slipped his hand to the small of her back and pulled Bridgette closer still.

Luke bent to her. His lips hovered above Bridgette's. Their breath mingled, becoming one.

The door opened with a bang. "Are you two in here?" Neil called out. "Mom needs the serving stuff and we all want another beer."

Bridgette slipped out of Luke's arms at the same moment her brother entered the kitchen.

Neil stopped short. Drawing his brows together, he asked, "What's going on here?"

Sure, Bridgette was a grown woman. It was also true that Luke had dated her when they were in high school. It was also a fact that nobody—Neil included—wanted to see their sister kissed by any dude.

"Um..." said Luke.

"Who got hurt?" Neil asked, gesturing to the first-aid kit and bloodied towel.

"I cut my finger," said Bridgette, holding up her injury as proof. "Dry off the flatware and I'll finish up. Luke, beer's in the fridge, help yourself."

Had she really let the moment slip away in an instant? Was Bridgette's heart racing like Luke's? Or had she not been moved by the moment at all?

Bridgette stood alone in her parents' kitchen. From the window, she had a clear view of the entire lawn that sloped down to the lake.

Everyone had gathered around the table, bathed in the glow of a dozen candles. Her eye was drawn to Luke, and her lips began to tingle with the kiss that never happened. In the quiet kitchen, Bridgette admitted, if only to herself, that she was attracted to Luke.

It was more than his blue eyes, or strong arms, or broad shoulders, or tight ass, that drew her in. It was him. His smile. His willingness to lend a hand, no matter the personal inconvenience. Like the old saying went, they didn't make them like Luke Walker anymore.

Then again, could she really give her heart away again?

Hadn't Bridgette learned her lesson? Everyone she ever truly loved would one day die.

The back door opened and closed. "Bridgette. Are you still in here?" called Jordana.

"In the kitchen."

"What's keeping you?" Jordana asked. "You know Mom won't let anyone eat until we're all together, and no offense, but I'm starving."

"I didn't mean to keep people waiting. Let's go."

Jordana said, "Wait a second. You look spooked. What's the matter? Is it because your car was vandalized?"

"I'm fine," said Bridgette. "But let's go. I really don't want people hungry on my account."

Without a word, they walked out of the house and across the patio.

"Why are you so jumpy tonight?" Jordana asked.

"Why are you so nosy?"

"I'm your big sister and a cop. It's kind of my job."

Bridgette gave a quiet laugh. "Coming back home has made me realize how many secrets we try to bury in the past."

"Like how you feel about Luke Walker?"

"Jeez, that's pretty blunt."

"Like I said, I'm your big sister and a cop. Being blunt comes with the territory, too."

"For your information, I don't feel any way about Luke."

"You used to."

"Yes, as in the past. Besides, I'm still not sure how I feel about Henry."

"You loved your husband." Jordana placed her hand on Bridgette's shoulder and pulled her to a stop. "But he really is in the past. Luke Walker is right here, and I can see how he looks at you. How you look at him."

Despite herself, Bridgette scanned the group gathered around the bonfire. Luke was talking to her father and brother, Ty. Looking up, his gaze met hers. He lifted his beer in a salute. She waved back.

"See?"

"No," said Bridgette, shrugging off her sister's touch. "I don't see anything."

She stalked away, thankful to leave the conversation behind. Especially since Jordana had been right. Luke had awakened emotions in Bridgette she thought had died with her husband.

Chapter 10

Night draped its velvety cloak over the sky. The meal had been served and enjoyed. After the table was cleared, dessert was brought out—an obvious choice of a s'mores bar. Luke watched Bridgette and Yvette catch their marshmallows on fire and then giggle, much like schoolgirls.

"Hey, Luke," said Brooks. "I'd like to introduce you to my girlfriend, Gwen Harrison."

Gwen, a lithe redhead with a warm smile, held out her hand to shake. "It's a pleasure to meet you."

Dex, cocktail in hand, stood nearby and snorted.

Brooks rounded on the older man. "What in the hell is your problem?"

"You know you can do better, right?" Dex asked.

"What'd you say?" Narrowing his eyes, Brooks stepped forward.

Holding up a hand, Dex slurped his drink. "My boy, I've been around a long time and I know a tart when I see one."

"Tart?" Brooks lunged forward.

Luke didn't think; he acted. Stepping between the two men, he placed his palms on Brooks's chest. "Calm down, man."

Brooks tried to brush his hand aside. "You heard what Dex said to Gwen. How am I supposed to be calm?"

The chatter from the other partygoers fell away, leaving the night completely silent except for the crackling bonfire.

"It's late," said Luke. "Everyone is tired. Dex has been drinking. But you're right, he was out of line."

Brooks tried to step forward again. "He is out of line and someone needs to put him back."

Luke, his hand still on Brooks's chest, shoved him back a little. "How is getting into a fight with your dad's business partner going to make things better? Is Gwen going to like you more? What about your mom? Or your sisters? Do they need to see you get violent?"

Brooks, a bowstring pulled tight, let the tension lessen. "I guess not."

"Then come on," said Luke. "Go roast a marshmallow. Everyone will feel better with something sweet."

Dex, seemingly oblivious to the problem he'd caused, walked away.

Brooks nodded and turned to Gwen. "You okay?"

"I'm shocked," she said. "Offended. I've never met Markus Dexter before, so I don't know why he has a problem with me."

"Dex is the problem," said Brooks.

Luke took that as his cue to give the new couple a moment alone. He walked away from the bonfire and into the darkness.

"Luke, wait." He didn't have to turn around to know who'd spoken. It was Bridgette. Slowing his gait, he waited as she jogged to his side. "Where are you going?"

"I guess I just needed a minute alone."

"Everyone can be overwhelming, that's for sure," Bridgette said. "It's part of the reason I wanted to live in town. I need quiet, and sometimes it's impossible to think around here."

She paused. He said nothing. His gaze on the ground, Luke gave a noncommittal nod.

After a moment, she continued, "I just wanted to make sure you're okay and thank you for stepping in. You did a great job defusing a situation that could've gotten real ugly real fast."

He dug the toe of his shoe through the grass. "You're welcome," he said.

She stood at his side a moment longer.

What did Bridgette want? What should he say? Should he bring up what happened in the kitchen? Should he try to kiss her again?

"Well," she said with a sigh. "I don't want to interrupt your time alone."

Bridgette turned to go. He should just let her walk away. True, Luke's life was far from exciting, but

Bridgette came with complications. More than the feelings she aroused in him, she had a large and messy family. Moreover, if his guess was right, she was still dealing with her grief after the death of her spouse. Wasn't he content with his dull, predictable life? Hadn't he had enough drama as a kid while dealing with his father's illness?

If all of that was true, why did he call to Bridgette? "You know, you can stay if you want. We can be alone together."

She laughed and the sound filled his chest. "If we're together, then we wouldn't be alone, would we?"

"I suppose not," said Luke. "But I really do like your company. In fact, I don't know of anyone else I'd rather be with."

"Oh," she said. She stepped backward as if surprised by what he'd said. "That's quite a compliment."

"It's true."

"Until earlier this week, we hadn't spoken in decades. You can't know anything about me. I could have changed."

"You haven't changed that much, Bridgette."

She shook her head. "I'm not so sure about that."

A burst of laughter erupted from the party. Whatever issues had been brewing before seemed to have been forgotten.

"Have you had any luck getting an animal shelter involved in the Boo-fest parade?"

"To be honest, I haven't had time. The beginning of each case is always involved. But I promise to look into it tomorrow."

"I wasn't pressuring you," said Luke. "Just asking because I want the downtown festival to be worthwhile. Who knows, maybe we can expand to the winter holidays or do something for spring."

"Sounds like you really love the town."

"Of course," said Luke. "It's my home. Don't you love Braxville, too?"

She shrugged. "Like you said, it's home. But *love*? I don't know. It seems like there are so many things I didn't notice when I lived here last."

"Like what?"

"Well, I'm sure you heard, but two bodies were found on one of the old construction sites."

"I heard about that," said Luke. "Do the police know anything?"

"You'd have to ask Yvette," said Bridgette. "She's the one working on the case."

Luke knew he never would but nodded. "Is that it? Are there any other secrets lurking in the darkness?"

Bridgette shrugged again. "Maybe."

Her evasive answer covered Luke's arms with gooseflesh. *Maybe?* "How's your work? What brought you to Braxville?"

"There's a cluster of cancer cases in town. Several men have developed esophageal cancer. Statistically, it's impossible for all of these cases to be random."

She kept talking, but her words grew faint, as if she were faraway. His chest tightened, making it hard to breathe. "Esophageal cancer?"

"That's what I said." Bridgette laid her hand on

Luke's shoulder. "Are you okay? You look like you're about to get sick."

A bead of sweat trickled down the side of Luke's face. He wiped it away. "My dad was sick, back when we were kids."

"Yeah," said Bridgette. "I remember." Even in the dark, Luke could tell that the color drained from her face. "Oh, no. Don't tell me that your father had esophageal cancer."

"He did."

"Luke, I'm positive that the state hasn't identified him as being part of the cluster. Still, it's my job. I have to speak to him."

"I can arrange that. What should I do? Bring my dad to your office? Do you want to come to his house?"

Bridgette glanced over her shoulder and looked back at the party. Suddenly Luke wanted nothing more than to go home.

"My family owns a fishing cabin on Lake Kanopolis," Bridgette said.

Luke remembered the property well. He'd lost his virginity to Bridgette under a cottonwood on that very same lake. "I know."

"We can go there tomorrow morning. It'll give us some privacy."

"Can we make it after two o'clock in the afternoon? That's when the store closes for the weekend," he said. There were so many other thoughts taking shape in his mind. Things he wanted to say but shouldn't. Things he wanted to ask for but wouldn't.

"Two o'clock works just fine," she said. "Let's go back before someone comes looking for us."

"Hold on for one more minute," said Luke. Sure, he was about to step over the line, but tonight he didn't care. "What can you tell me about the cancer cases?"

"At the moment, not much."

"Is that because it's confidential."

"Right now," said Bridgette, "I'm just trying to understand what all the victims have in common. It's that one thread—a simple thin thread—that will run through the life of each man. We will find that thread and follow it until it leads us to the cause."

"You know, my dad was diagnosed with cancer when I was just a kid. In a way, I lost my childhood to the disease. For a long time, I was mad. Mad at my dad for getting sick. Mad at my mom for needing me to take on extra responsibilities around the house. Mad at God for letting everything happen. Mad at myself for, well, being so damned angry." He paused and drew in a breath. "But I really didn't think there was anyone to blame."

Luke tilted his head back. Stars, a thousand pinpricks of light, shone through the eternal blackness of the night sky. "And now you're telling me that someone or something might be at the root of all this suffering?"

"I want to be very careful with what I say next, Luke. I don't know that your father belongs in the cancer cluster." She sighed. "From what you've told me, there's enough evidence for me to investigate further. That's it."

"I have no right to ask this of you, Bridgette," Luke began. "Promise me that you'll figure out what's happening in Braxville. Even after all these years, you're still the smartest person I know."

"Getting to the bottom of all of these cases is why I'm here," she said. "It's my job and I will make things right for everyone in town."

He took a step toward her. And then another. And another. Luke was so close that he could hear her breathing and see the pulse thrumming at the base of her neck. "Promise me," said Luke, "that you'll find out what happened in our home. Find out what happened to my father."

She looked down. For a single moment, time stopped and Luke was positive that she was going to refuse his request.

What had he been thinking? He never should have asked anything of her, yet he had. And once Bridgette said no? Well, would he ever be able to face her again?

"For you, I promise to do my best and never give up," she said.

"Your best is more than enough," said Luke.

Still, she stood close. All he had to do was lift a finger and he would touch her. He remembered the feel of her skin. She'd been soft and warm. In her arms, he came to understand what it meant to be a man. And it had nothing to do with discovering sex. Being a man meant protecting those you loved. It meant showing up even if you didn't feel like it. It meant always being an example worth following.

Another burst of laughter erupted from the party. Bridgette looked over her shoulder and the moment was gone.

"Come on," she said. "Let's make a s'more before everything's gone."

Without speaking, they returned to the party. Luke had been so focused on their past that he hadn't actually realized what he wanted from Bridgette. But he knew now.

It was a future.

Then again, Bridgette was still a grieving widow. Did that make Luke a fool for wanting more?

The flat tires on her car and the tussle between Brooks and Dex notwithstanding, Bridgette considered the annual Colton bonfire a success. In fact, she was sincerely sorry when the evening ended, and not counting the minutes until the family event was over.

As she waved goodbye to her parents, Bridgette realized that she hadn't spoken to either one about Colton Construction's possible connection to the cancer cases. Sure, she'd been distracted by Luke, but really, Bridgette knew there was more.

She felt as if she were trapped between the proverbial rock and a hard place. She didn't want to upset her parents or seem disloyal to the family.

Then again, several of the men in her investigation were former employees of Colton Construction. It wasn't a detail she could ignore. In fact, she'd be neglecting her duty if she didn't investigate.

With Luke at her side, they returned to his truck. He opened the passenger door and Bridgette slid into the seat. After rounding to the driver's side and getting in, he started the engine and drove down the long drive and took the road back to Braxville.

"I was thinking about tomorrow," said Luke. "If you want, we can ride together. No sense in taking two cars."

"Especially since mine might not be fixed yet," she added.

"True," said Luke with a nod.

Headlights sliced through the night and the outside world passed in a shadowy blur. The purr of the engine and the rumbling truck were enough to lull Bridgette into a trance.

"About your car," said Luke.

"Yeah," she mumbled as her stupor neared sleep.

"I think I know what happened. What I don't know is why."

Adrenaline rushed through her veins. She sat up. "What do you mean?"

"Do you remember the woman you saw on the street the other night?"

"Your ex-girlfriend? Julia?"

"That's the one."

"What about her?"

"After you came over, I called her mother and told her that Julia had been hanging out at all hours. Her mother was shocked. Julia said she had been at work. I think Julia was upset that I'd contacted her mother, and slashing your tires was retaliation. What I don't get is why would she vandalize your car? Why not damage my truck?"

"That might not be much of a mystery," said

Bridgette. "I saw her at the coffee shop the next morning when I grabbed breakfast for the two of us. Megan said your name when I picked up the order. Julia overheard, I'm sure of it."

"And then?" Luke coaxed.

Bridgette's face burned with a blush. Thank goodness the cabin was dark. "And then I told Julia that you and I dated in high school."

"Is that all you said? And how did that come up in conversation, anyway?"

"I might have let her believe that I spent the night with you, as well."

"You what?" Luke jerked the wheel as he gaped at her. They rumbled over the shoulder, kicking up a cloud of dust. Righting the truck, he smiled and shook his head. "I can't believe you implied that we'd been together. What were you thinking?"

"I guess that was the problem," she said. "I wasn't thinking at all." Bridgette stared out the window at the miles and miles of plains that stretched out forever.

How could she have been so stupid with Julia? Speaking to Luke's ex had been a rash decision that went against her cautious and thoughtful nature. "I was trying to help," she began. "You told me that she'd been lurking around your store for months. I hoped that if she thought you'd moved on, then she'd do the same."

"If she's the one who flattened your tires, I'd say she hasn't moved on at all."

"Obviously not," said Bridgette. "I didn't mean to make matters worse, but it seems like I have."

"Julia's never been destructive before," said Luke.

"The fact that I don't know what else she might do bothers me."

"It does a hell of a lot more than bother me." She leaned back in the seat and rubbed away the tension between her brow. "Maybe it would be best if I just moved back to my parents' house."

"You can if you want, but I was thinking of something else."

"What else can I do? Are there other apartments to rent in Braxville?"

Luke stared straight ahead and worked his jaw back and forth. "Well," he began. "You can stay with me."

Julia drove in the dark. The headlights on Luke's truck cut a wedge out of the darkness. Yet driving without lights—or even being seen by Luke—wasn't Julia's main concern. It was Bridgette Colton. The other woman's silhouette was unmistakable in the passenger seat.

Hands trembling, Julia gripped the steering wheel so tight that she feared it would break. Sweat dripped down the back of her shirt. Her head throbbed and her stomach roiled. But it was no malady of the body.

Julia was stricken with disbelief and heartache.

Were Luke and Bridgette really an item?

Luke had taken Bridgette to her parents' house. He'd stayed. He was bringing her home. It was almost as if they were on a date. Had Julia caused this to happen? Had her ploy to get Bridgette to move back home only brought her closer to Luke?

It seemed impossible. Yet, in front of her, in the cabin of Luke's truck was the proof. As they drew closer to

Braxville, subdivisions branched off the main road. Above, streetlamps spilled pools of light across the asphalt, giving off enough illumination for Luke to see her car.

If he did, what then?

She didn't want a repeat of the encounter with her mother. Letting her foot off the accelerator, Julia turned into a nearby neighborhood. Small houses sat behind chain link fences. In the distance, a dog barked.

Julia found a house that was dark except for a sconce above the door, and she parked at the end of the drive. Turning off the ignition, she leaned back in her seat. She had time to wait. She knew where he was going.

What she didn't know: Was there anything beyond friendship between Luke and Bridgette? She intended to find out.

Chapter 11

As Luke turned his truck onto Main Street in downtown Braxville, Bridgette was exhausted both in body and spirit. Seemingly, a million different problems filled her mind. A night of uninterrupted sleep would help her sort out the answers.

But there was one issue that she couldn't escape.

How did she feel about Luke?

Bridgette glanced at him as he drove. Silvery light from the dashboard turned the angles of his face sharper, his eyes a deeper shade of blue. In the light, his lips were the color of spilled wine and she imagined the feeling of his mouth on hers.

This was no adolescent memory.

It was an all-too-real adult fantasy. Her pulse began to race, and Bridgette looked away.

"What's on your mind?" he asked.

Damn. He'd caught her staring. What was she supposed to say now? "I was just thinking about how Braxville looks exactly the same as it did when I was a kid. In reality, everything is different."

"Or maybe you're just noticing new things for the first time," he said.

"Maybe," said Bridgette as Luke parked his truck at the curb. His grille was next to her rear bumper. "Will my car be safe here tonight? I'll have it towed in the morning."

"I hope so," he said. "Like I said, usually crime is low in Braxville."

True, she and Luke were having a conversation. So far, neither one of them had said much of anything. Although the air in the cabin was warm, the hair on Bridgette's arm stood on end. She glanced at Luke again. Her eyes were immediately drawn to his lips a second time.

Luke interrupted the silence. "I meant what I said before. You can stay in my apartment if you'd like. My sofa is comfortable enough." He paused. "I promise not to be a slob in the bathroom."

Bridgette laughed. "I'm sure you'd make a fabulous roommate."

"So you'll stay with me?"

"I moved out of my parents' house because I'm a grown woman and I need my own place. How would moving in with you keep me independent?"

"It's more for your safety," he said.

"I know," said Bridgette. "Truly, I do. I appreciate

your concern and offer. But you're right across the hall. If I need anything, I can come to you."

"Of course," said Luke. "At least let me look through your apartment and make sure everything's in order."

Bridgette wasn't sure if Luke's precautions were justified or not. "Thanks," she said. "That'd be great."

In less than a minute, they stood in front of Bridgette's apartment. She opened the door. The room beyond was dark as pitch. Luke flipped a wall switch and a table lamp glowed, filling the room with light.

A blanket was draped across the end of the sofa. A plate, filled with crumbs from her morning bagel, sat on the kitchen counter. A mug, with the dregs of her coffee, sat in the middle of the plate. "It looks like it did when I left for work," she said.

"Mind if I check out the bedroom and the bath?"

Bridgette hadn't unpacked, much less made a mess worthy of embarrassment. "Help yourself," she said.

Luke disappeared through the single door and she moved to the window. Bracing her palms on the sill, she looked down onto the street below.

Luke said that Julia had been lurking outside his store for months.

Was she watching them now?

"Everything looks good," he said, stepping into the living room.

Bridgette used the mirrored glass and looked at Luke without turning around. "Thanks again for checking out my apartment. And for driving me to my parents'. And staying at the bonfire, even though my family can be nutty."

Luke slipped the tips of his fingers into the pockets of his jeans. "Everyone's family is a little crazy. Still, you Coltons are good people."

Bridgette wasn't sure how to respond and returned her gaze to the street below. She half expected to see Julia standing on the sidewalk, but the road was empty.

"Well, I better get going," said Luke. "Tomorrow's a busy day at the store."

Maybe it was just a bunch of kids who'd flattened her tires. Maybe the destruction had been random. Maybe Julia had nothing to do with the damage done to Bridgette's car. If that was the case, why did Bridgette suddenly loathe the idea of being left alone? "Let me make you a cup of tea," she said. "It's the least I can do."

"The food and the company tonight were more than enough, but thanks."

"Sure," she said, turning back to the window. "It's late. I understand."

There, just across the street, in the recessed entrance to a hair salon, Bridgette saw something. Movement? A flash of color where there should only be shadows? She sucked in a breath. With her pulse racing, she took a step back.

"What?" Luke asked as he moved to her. He was so close that his chest brushed against her back. She liked the heat from his body. Liked the feeling of his hard muscles next to her skin. Liked that being near Luke reminded Bridgette of what it meant to be a woman.

He asked, "What is it?"

"I'm not sure," said Bridgette. "I thought I saw something."

She moved back to the window. Her breath fogged the glass, and she wiped it away with her sleeve. "In the doorway across the street, something caught my eye."

Luke stood behind her, his hand resting on the small of her back. "What'd you see?"

"That's just it. It was only a glimpse of…whatever. It startled me."

A cat darted out from the doorway and sprinted down the street, its fur gleaming in the streetlight.

Bridgette laughed. "I guess I did see something."

"Your property was damaged," said Luke. "It's totally natural to be on edge."

She pivoted where she stood, coming face-to-face with Luke. Her fingers itched with the need to touch him. She reached up and then paused with her palms halfway to his chest. What was she thinking?

Balling her hands into fists, Bridgette forced her arms to her side.

"You know," said Luke, moving closer to her. "I might just take that cup of tea."

"Let me put water on to boil," she said, yet she didn't move.

"Maybe you should," he said. His voice was low and deep, and sent reverberations through her chest. He leaned to her. His breath washed over her cheek.

She moved closer still. Their lips were close but not yet touching.

Then Bridgette reached up and ran her fingers through the short hairs at the nape of Luke's neck.

"Are you sure you want to do this again? Get involved with me?"

"To be honest," said Bridgette, "there's only one thing I know. Only one thing that I want."

"Oh, yeah?" he asked. "What's that?"

"I want you," she said, "to kiss me."

Bridgette's invitation was all Luke needed. His mouth was on hers, and his world shrank until it filled the apartment, and Luke and Bridgette were the only two people who mattered.

Moving his hand from her back upward to her hair, he wrapped his fingers in her long tresses. Luke pulled back on her head, exposing her throat. He licked her neck. Sucked on her earlobe. When she let out a mew of delight, he returned his lips to hers. Slipping his tongue inside her mouth, Luke explored, tasted and conquered.

"Luke," she said into his mouth, their breath becoming one. "Oh, Luke."

He pressed her into the window, his hand traveling from her hair to her stomach. He worked his fingers under the hem of her shirt, just to see if she felt as soft as he imagined.

She was.

His fingers traveled farther up her stomach, and the tips of his fingers grazed the lace of her bra. Luke pressed against the fly of his jeans. He wanted Bridgette. And it wasn't just tonight. He'd always wanted her. Hers was the face that came to him in dreams and fantasies alike.

And then the window exploded. Glass rained down as a piece of concrete skittered across the floor. Luke went numb for the span of a heartbeat. Time slowed as he recognized danger. Pulling Bridgette away from the window, they dropped to the floor. He covered her with his body.

"What the hell just happened?" she asked.

Luke didn't have an answer. Rising up, he glanced out of the window. The street was empty—except for a lone figure running down the road.

Even from his vantage point, he could clearly see the retreating form. Moreover, he knew exactly who had broken the window.

It was Julia.

"Son of a bitch," Luke growled. His hands shook with rage. He'd honestly tried to be reasonable with her, and it hadn't done either one of them any good.

"What's going on, Luke?" Bridgette asked, her eyes wide. "What happened?"

Holding out his hand, he pulled Bridgette to her feet. "It was Julia. Looks like she threw a piece of concrete through the window." Bits of glass sparkled in Bridgette's hair. He dusted them away. "Are you hurt?"

She drew in a shaking breath. "Just startled, that's all."

"I don't know what to say," he said. "Obviously, I knew that Julia had an unhealthy attachment, but I never imagined she'd be destructive, much less violent."

"I guess everyone's full of surprises," she said with a wry chuckle.

He supposed that Bridgette keeping some of her sense of humor was a good thing. Yet Julia's behavior was no laughing matter, especially since her animosity was directed at Bridgette.

"Grab whatever you need for the night," said Luke.

"Why?"

"There's no way I'm letting you stay here alone. You can crash at my place tonight. Tomorrow, we can figure out what to do next."

Bridgette looked at the door leading to her bedroom, to the chunk of concrete on the floor, and then back at Luke. He could well imagine the arguments she was forming. She was a grown woman. Julia was now long gone. Even if Luke's ex came back, she couldn't get into the stairwell that led to the apartments.

Before she said a word, Luke held up his hand. "I don't want to fight with you, but I insist that you keep yourself out of harm's way. This apartment isn't safe for you—not tonight anyway."

To his surprise, Bridgette nodded her head. "You're right. Give me a minute and I'll be right back."

And then Luke was alone. He pulled the phone from his pocket and placed a call that he had never intended to make. It was answered after the second ring. "This is Detective Reese Carpenter."

"Hey, it's Luke Walker. I have a problem and I need your help."

Bridgette needed only a few minutes to pack an overnight bag. She returned to the living room and set the bag on the floor. Luke stared at her, his jaw tight.

"Everything okay?" she asked.

"You know Reese Carpenter?"

"Of course. He's Jordana's partner on the police force."

"I called him about Julia," he said. "At first, I thought she was only lovesick, but this is more than I can deal with—and I definitely can't ignore what she's done. Not when she's threatening you."

Bridgette wasn't sure how to feel. Was she terrified that she was now a target of Luke's ex-girlfriend? Or was she touched by Luke's caring and concern?

Like always, Bridgette needed more information.

"What's Reese going to do?"

"Come here," said Luke. "I suppose he'll get pictures of the damage. Take a report. And, most important, he's going to talk to Julia." Whatever he was about to say next was interrupted by the pinging of a message on his phone. Luke glanced at the screen. "He's here. You'll be okay while I let him in?"

"Of course," said Bridgette, though her heart raced at the idea of being alone even for a few seconds. Folding her arms across her chest, she continued, "Go ahead. I'm fine."

Luke didn't bother to shut the front door, and the sound of his footsteps on the staircase were unmistakable.

"Thanks for coming, man," said Luke as he opened the door.

Bridgette recognized Reese's deep voice. He replied, "It's my job. Let's chat here for a minute. Can you tell me anything more than what you said on the phone?"

"Not really. Julia, the woman I dated over the summer, continued to hang around after we broke up. I told her to stop. She didn't. I figured she'd have to get bored eventually and go away, right?"

"I'm guessing that you were wrong."

"Bridgette Colton rented the apartment across the hall on Tuesday."

Reese asked, "As in Jordana's little sister?"

"The same. Anyway, Julia has taken a great disliking to Bridgette. Earlier, all four of Bridgette's tires had been slashed. Then tonight, someone threw a brick through Bridgette's window."

"Someone?"

"I saw Julia running down the street."

"But you didn't see her throw the concrete."

"No," he said. "But it's not hard to figure out what happened."

Reese asked, "And you didn't see her tampering with Bridgette's car, either. Correct?"

"You're correct," said Luke.

"Since you didn't see what happened to either the car or the window, I can't charge Julia with anything," said Reese. "What I can do is ask around. Maybe some of your neighbors or the other business owners saw something."

"If they didn't? What then? Are you saying that Julia will just get away with what she's done? Believe me, I know she's guilty. I have all the proof I need," said Luke.

"Calm down, man. There's a few things I can do with Julia even if I'm not going to arrest her or charge her with a crime."

"Like what?" Luke asked.

"I'll run her name through the system and see if she has any outstanding warrants."

"I doubt she does," said Luke. "So, what happens after that?"

Reese continued, "If she doesn't have a record, I'll stop by her house and have a chat. Hopefully, a visit from the police will help her to understand the seriousness of her behavior."

"Hopefully?" Luke echoed. "I just want to make sure that Bridgette is safe, you know."

"You two used to date, isn't that right?" asked Reese.

"Back in high school," said Luke.

"Is she the ex-girlfriend who got you all worked up the other night?"

Luke mumbled something that Bridgette couldn't hear. He continued, "She was my first love and is still a special lady. It's my job to keep her safe."

"That's noble of you," said the detective. "But I'm the expert in safety. Let's take a look at the damage. Then I'll talk to Julia."

Treading lightly, Bridgette moved across the room and shut the door. Undoubtedly, she hadn't been meant to overhear the conversation between Luke and Reese Carpenter. Then again, what was she supposed to do with what she now knew?

Did Luke really have feelings for her?

And what about the kiss?

Bridgette had spent the last two years clinging to the past. Now she had no idea how to feel about having a future. Especially one that might include Luke Walker.

Julia feared that she would retch. How could she have been so stupid?

In all honesty, she didn't even remember throwing the damned piece of concrete—a chunk of sidewalk that had broken loose. Hell, she barely remembered picking it up.

All she recalled was the weight of the slab in her hand. The rough edges biting into her palm. The heat of anger consuming her as Luke embraced Bridgette.

Then the concrete went airborne. As it sailed across the street, Julia had felt a sense of relief, as if she truly had launched her fury. It slammed through the window and she froze for an instant.

Christ, who knew that she had such power and aim?

Without a backward glance, she'd sprinted from the scene. What else was she supposed to do?

Had she done more damage than breaking the window?

Had Luke been cut by a shard of glass? Had the heavy concrete hit Bridgette?

Julia pulled into her driveway, opened the car door, leaned out and emptied her stomach. Everything she'd eaten splattered across the ground. Wiping away the last of her spittle with a fast-food napkin, she asked herself again how she could have been so stupid.

The flickering light from the TV filtered around the edges of shades drawn over the front window. Damn. Despite the late hour, her mother was awake. Julia had messed up badly.

Would her mother be able to tell?

And if she could, what would she do?

Turning off the ignition, Julia stepped from the car. Her legs ached with each stride as she walked to the house.

"That you, Julia?" her mother called from the adjacent living room.

Julia busied herself with hanging up her coat and her purse, not daring to look in her mother's direction. "It is, Momma."

"Have fun at your friend's house?"

"I did, Momma," said Julia. "I'm going to get some dinner and go to bed, though. I'm real tired."

"Dinner? I thought you said that you were going to a barbecue."

Is that what she'd told her mother? Damn, Julia couldn't remember what she'd said. Sure, just a few hours had passed, yet it seemed like days since she'd last spoken to her mother. "It was, but the sauce didn't sit right with me."

"I didn't make you a plate," her mother said. "But if you give me a minute, I can get you a sandwich."

"Don't worry," Julia interrupted. "I'm just going to grab a bowl of cereal, or something."

Outside, a car's engine idled.

The neighbor's dog barked.

Julia, standing next to the coatrack, froze.

Of course, someone could be outside for a million different reasons. Yet, Julia's palms began to tingle, and she knew the truth. She'd been seen by Luke or Bridgette. They'd called the police.

Tonight was not going to end well.

She opened the front door again. There, at the curb, was a Braxville Police Department cruiser. A man with dark hair sat in the driver's seat.

Julia stepped outside.

"Where are you going?" her mother called after her.

"I forgot something in the car," Julia yelled over her shoulder. "I'll be right back."

"Are you going outside without your coat?"

Julia shut the door on her mother's question.

Standing on the stoop, she waited as the man stepped from his vehicle. "Are you Julia?"

For a moment, she considered lying though she knew better. Her ruse, once discovered, would only make matters worse. She gave a quick nod of her head. "I am."

"I'm Detective Reese Carpenter, with the Braxville Police. Can I ask where you were tonight?"

"I know what I did was wrong," she began. "And honestly, I'm sorry."

"What did you do that was wrong?" he asked.

Did he want her to confess? Or was the police officer here for an entirely different reason? Had she already said too much? No. Detective Carpenter coming to her house was no coincidence. The more honest she was, the better it would be. Wasn't that what the doctors at the hospital always said?

"I got mad and threw a chunk of concrete at a window. I'm pretty sure the window broke, but I started running as soon as I heard the crack."

"Anything else?"

Well, she was in for a penny, she might as well be in for a pound. "I sliced the tires on Bridgette Colton's car," she said, suddenly too tired to lie anymore. "I dated Luke Walker over the summer. I really thought that he was the one. We broke up and, well, he started dating someone else. Like I said, I was upset."

"You know that destroying property is a crime? You can be criminally charged for what you did tonight."

"I know," said Julia. Tears burned her eyes. Would crying help her cause? "I really am sorry. I'll pay for the damages, if that helps."

"You may very well end up being sent a bill, but that's not for me to decide." The police officer exhaled. "What I want is for you to stay far away from both Luke Walker and Bridgette Colton. If I hear that you've bothered either one of them, even a little, I'm coming back. Our chat will be different next time. You won't receive a warning, and when I leave, you'll be coming to the station with me. Got it?"

"Got it," said Julia. Was that it? Of their own accord, the corners of her mouth turned up. She pressed her thumb to her lips, hiding the smile.

"Try to have yourself a good night and remember what I said."

"I'll stay away from Luke and Bridgette."

The police officer drew in a long breath and opened his mouth, ready to say something else. With a shake of his head, he slipped back into his car and closed the door. As he drove away, Julia's knees went weak. She held on to her house for support, thankful that there'd been no real consequences.

Turning, Julia opened the door and stepped inside. Her mother—and her wheelchair—blocked the entryway. Even in the darkness, Julia could see that her mother's mouth was pressed into a colorless line.

"Was everything that I just heard true? Did you really break a window and flatten somebody's tires?"

"If you heard all that," Julia began. Her hands went numb and the back of her knees began to sweat. "Then you heard me say that I was sorry. You heard me admit that I'd gotten mad and also promise not to bother Luke anymore."

"What about his girlfriend?"

Julia recalled the scene on the windowsill. Bridgette's mouth pressed onto Luke's like a sucker fish on a dirty tank. Julia's face burned as her chest filled with shame and rage. "Her, too."

"You have to listen to the police officer, Julia. There are worse places to go than the hospital."

Julia snorted. "I doubt it."

"Like jail," said her mother. "Jail's worse than a hospital."

"I know, Momma," she said, leaning on the wall. "I'm going to bed now."

"I thought you were hungry. What happened to having some cereal?"

"I've lost my appetite," she said, pushing from thc wall and walking down the short hallway.

"You need to be careful," said her mother.

Laying her hand on the doorknob, Julia turned. The TV was still on. Light spilled into the entryway, casting her mother in flickering shadows. "I'll be careful," Julia said.

"And you need to leave Luke Walker alone. You know that."

Julia opened the door to her room. "I heard the police officer," she said. "And I heard you." With that, she pushed the door shut and turned on the light. Luke's face was on every inch of her wall. Tracing a finger over a picture, she spoke. "You don't have to worry," she said. "I won't abandon you."

Chapter 12

Bridgette woke in a bed that she knew wasn't hers. In an instant, moments from last night came back like a wave crashing against the shore. Her car being vandalized. The party at her parents. The kiss with Luke. The brick coming through the window. The visit by the police. And, finally, the arrangement for her to stay at Luke's apartment, at least until the window was fixed.

Luke insisted that Bridgette take his room and she'd been too tired to argue. Like a gentleman, he slept on the sofa. She inhaled. The sheets smelled like fresh-cut lumber, spice and the out-of-doors. They smelled like Luke.

Dropping her feet to the floor, Bridgette stood. She twisted her tresses into a bun and secured her hair in place with a band. With one more stretch, she wandered from the bedroom. The living room and adjacent kitchen were empty, and a single sheet of paper sat in the middle of the coffee table.

It was a note from Luke.

His handwriting had changed little over the years.

Good morning, his note began. Bridgette smiled, imagining that he was far too chipper for the early hour.

I'm at work but help yourself to anything you find in the kitchen. Coffee's fresh. There are towels in the bathroom. Stop by if you get bored. I'll see you this afternoon.

She set the note back on the table, inexplicably sad she had woken up to an empty apartment.

With an entire morning to fill, she made a plan: First things first and she called a local garage to collect her car. After arrangements for a garage to tow her car had been made, she turned her attention to the Boo-fest. Thanks to Bridgette's old roommate, the Braxville Boo-fest was about to get help from a very popular TV show. More than that, Bridgette hoped to help some well-deserving pets find their forever home.

She read through the binder he'd been given and ninety minutes later, Bridgette had written a short press release. After that, she showered, got ready for the day and finished a Google search. With an address written on the back of her note, she locked the front door and descended the stairs to the street.

Walking past the hardware store, she peered into the window. More than a dozen customers stood in line at the counter. She was happy to see the place so busy. All the same, she'd hoped to catch a glimpse of Luke.

Pressing her lips together, she recalled the feeling of his mouth on hers and a shiver of desire danced along her skin. What would have happened last night if Luke's ex hadn't shattered the window?

Then again, Bridgette knew. She'd have woken up with him in the bed, not on the sofa.

It brought up another question. How would she have felt about their lovemaking this morning? Was Luke a mistake she'd soon regret?

With a shake of her head, she started walking.

"Good morning," a voice called out. She recognized it at once and stopped. It was him.

The door to the hardware store was open and Luke stood on the threshold. "I wanted you to know that I got a text from Reese Carpenter," Luke said. "He stopped by Julia's house last night. She admitted to throwing the concrete that broke the window. She also said she was sorry for overreacting and promised to leave me—and you—alone."

"Thanks for the update," she said. "I'm glad that everything got sorted out with your ex."

Luke said, "Me, too." He paused. "Where are you headed?"

Bridgette looked at her note and read the address.

"Is that Perfect Pets Dog Shelter?"

"I want to see if we can get some of their dogs to participate in the parade."

"I'll go with you," said Luke. "I know the shelter's director."

Of course he knew the director. Luke Walker knew everyone in town. "What about your store. It looks busy."

"My dad helps out on Saturday mornings. He'll be okay for a few minutes."

Sure, having Luke help with introductions would be great. All the same, that meant they'd be spending more time together. It wasn't that she disliked Luke; in fact, it was the complete opposite. Luke was attractive, smart, considerate and hardworking. He was everything she admired in a man.

And that was the problem.

Luke was damn close to being perfect. And Bridgette was damn close to losing her heart to him again.

Would that be such a bad thing?

Then again, how would he feel once he knew why their sweet summer love had turned sour?

The morning sky was clear and bright blue, promising a sunny fall day. All the stores in the downtown were open and filled with patrons, leaving Luke more than a little pleased.

Perfect Pets Dog Shelter was located two blocks from the downtown shopping district, where businesses and residential properties started to blend. Located in a renovated Victorian mansion, a wooden cutout of a dog hung from a light pole at the gate.

"Here we are," said Luke, gesturing to the brick walkway.

Bridgette turned to the walkway and he followed her

to the porch. They opened the front door and the sound of happy barking greeted them.

Steven Faulkner, the director of the shelter, looked up from a reception desk that sat in the one-time foyer.

"Luke," said the older man, getting to his feet. "Good to see you. What brings you by today?"

Hand on Bridgette's back, Luke said, "Let me introduce you to my friend and the newest chair of the Boo-fest parade, Bridgette Colton."

"Colton, eh. Are you one of Fitz and Lilly's kids?"

Bridgette smiled and stepped forward. "I am," she said, shaking hands with Steven. "It's a pleasure to meet you."

Luke continued, "Bridgette has an idea for the Boo-fest parade, but we need your help."

"Well, you've got me intrigued," said the older man. "What can I do?"

Bridgette spent a few minutes outlining her plan of partnering with the shelter to have dogs attend the Boo-fest and participatc in thc paradc. She concluded with the opportunity to have them featured on the popular TV show, *Good Morning, Wichita.* As she ended her spcech, Bridgctte asked, "What do you think?"

Steven was nodding and smiling, which Luke assumed was a good sign. "I think that you've come up with a great way to get much needed exposure for the shelter. And even better, a way to get some of the animals into their forever homes. I'm sure we can have a few at the parade, provided we pick the right ones."

"Of course," said Bridgette. "We'd only want dogs who are comfortable with a crowd and lots of attention."

"Let me give you the grand tour." Pointing to a winding staircase that led to the second floor, Steven said, "I have an apartment upstairs and then also run a low-cost vet clinic on Thursday mornings."

"You're a veterinarian?" Bridgette asked.

"Semiretired. My wife, Helen, and I always wanted to run a dog sanctuary. So, when I sold my practice, we remodeled the house and opened the shelter."

"That's a great retirement story," said Bridgette. "Where's Helen now?"

"She's in Kansas City, Missouri. Our oldest daughter just gave birth to another baby. A grandson."

"Congratulations," said Luke as Steven beamed with pride.

"Anyhow," said Dr. Faulkner, "follow me." He ushered them through a set of metal doors that led to the back of the house. All the walls had been knocked down on the main floor, leaving a single room with more than a dozen pens lining each wall. Most of the pens were occupied with barking, happy dogs.

Kneeling next to the first pen, she reached her fingers through the wire door. "Hello, boy," she said. A white-and-black dog with a short coat sniffed her fingers.

"That's Pocco," said Steven. "He's as sweet a fella as there is, but a bit shy. I don't think he'd enjoy being a part of the parade."

Bridgette rubbed the dog's ears. "We won't stress you out, then. Will we, boy?"

"He's taken a liking to you," said Steven. "I'm glad

to see that. He's been at the shelter for months, mostly because he's wary of strangers."

"Pocco knows a friend when he meets one," said Bridgette.

Since her return to Braxville, Bridgette had appeared to be serious-minded and competent. She'd shared with him that she was in town to do a job and had no intention of failing. Yet, in that moment of her kneeling next to the dog's cage, Luke saw another version of Bridgette. One that was vulnerable, open and, above all, caring.

His chest filled with an emotion he dared not examine.

An hour later, Bridgette and Luke had a list of ten dogs with the personality needed to be in the parade. Bridgette had also texted her friend, the TV producer, pictures of the dogs, along with pertinent information—breed, age, gender, name.

On her way out of the shelter, Bridgette stopped once again to visit Pocco. "Goodbye, boy. I'll see you real soon."

The dog's tail was a blur and he gave a happy bark.

"He really does like you," said Steven. "I rarely get him to say anything."

"If you ever need a dog walker, I'll volunteer."

"I can always use the help," said Steven. "In fact, he's due for a stroll if you want to take him out now."

"I'd love to," said Bridgette.

Luke had promised his father that he wouldn't be gone long. He really should get back to work. Then again, he wasn't about to miss a chance to take a walk with Bridgette.

"Care for some company?" he asked.

"If you can spare the time."

"For Pocco," said Luke as Steven hooked a lead to the dog's collar. "Anything."

The sun rose in the sky, warming the air. Without speaking, they walked down the sidewalk and turned into a residential neighborhood. Nose to the ground, Pocco snuffled as he walked.

"Hopefully," said Bridgette, "Someone will adopt this guy, too. It breaks my heart to see a good dog go overlooked time and again."

"Sounds like you have a passion for helping shelter dogs."

"For the most part, they're uncomplicated creatures. All a dog wants is to have someone to love and to be loved in return." He sensed she had more to say and waited for her to speak. "Two years ago, I was in a very low place. When Henry died, I lost more than my husband. I'd lost my future, along with all the plans we'd made. I'd lost my past, too, because of the history we shared."

"You were out of hope," he said.

"I've never thought about it that way, but I guess you're right." They walked another block in silence. Bridgette spoke again. "I threw myself into work for several months. It's what I'm good at, after all. Yet, I knew I needed to do more. At the same time, being around people was exhausting."

"Is that when you started volunteering at your local shelter?"

"A lot of dogs make great company. With a dog, I can just be. At least they don't ask too many questions."

"And how are you doing now?"

Bridgette shrugged. "Before I came home, I thought I had balance in my life."

"You don't?"

"Let's just say that family can make things more complicated."

"What about plans for your future?" Luke asked. "Do you know what else you want from life?"

"No." She exhaled. "With Henry, I knew I wanted kids."

"What about now? Do you want kids? Do you want to get married again?"

Bridgette glanced at her smartwatch. "We better get Pocco back to the shelter. It's getting late."

He wasn't a fool. Luke knew that she wanted to get rid of him. And he also knew why. He'd asked too many questions—questions that Bridgette didn't want to answer.

They turned at the corner, rounding the block and heading back to the shelter. At the end of the street, he glimpsed the back of a blue sedan as it drove away.

His heart began to race. Had it been Julia? Was she still stalking him despite being visited by the police?

The trip from Braxville to Lake Kanopolis took less than thirty minutes. For the entire drive, Paul Walker regaled Bridgette with stories, much to her delight and Luke's embarrassment.

"And then there was the one time we went hiking," said Mr. Walker. "Luke was about three years old. He'd stopped wearing diapers and there was no bathroom for miles. So, when he had to go, there was only the woods."

"Thanks, Dad," said Luke. For comfort's sake, they'd taken Paul's SUV. Luke drove. His father sat in the passenger seat and Bridgette rode in the back. "That's enough personal history for the day. Remember, Bridgette and I went to school together from kindergarten to graduation. She doesn't want to hear all of this."

"No, you can keep telling me about Luke," said Bridgette. "I didn't know him when he was in preschool. The stories are cute."

"Don't forget humiliating," added Luke.

Using the rearview mirror, she stole a glance at him. Sun shone on his face, turning his skin golden. Bridgette could almost pretend that the outing to the fishing cabin was just that—an outing. But she couldn't ignorc Luke's connection—through his father—to her investigation.

"Well," said Mr. Walker. "If you really don't want me to, then I guess I won't."

Luke exhaled. "Fine, finish the story."

Mr. Walker smiled. "Where were we?"

"In the woods and without a bathroom," Bridgette said.

"That's just it," said Mr. Walker. "My wife had worked so hard to get Luke potty trained that he wouldn't do anything because he wasn't in a bathroom."

"Uh-oh. What happened?"

"We convinced him that it was okay because it was outside, which made everyone happier that day."

"I feel like there was another day when people weren't as happy," said Bridgette.

"You'd be right. Like the next day, when my wife took him to the park."

Bridgette started laughing. "Oh, no."

Luke was laughing, too. "Oh, yes."

Luke turned up the long drive leading to the fishing cabin. Sun shone on the water, and Lake Kanopolis sparkled like a carpet of diamonds. Pulling up next to the back door, Luke put the SUV in Park.

Using a key that she'd gotten from her mother, Bridgette opened the back door. An alarm started beeping. She entered the code—Yvette's birthday, something everyone could remember.

The house, used every weekend in the summer, had been closed for the colder months ahead. Shades were drawn, leaving the interior dim. Sheets were draped over the furnishings. The air was stale and cold.

"Come on in," said Bridgette.

Paul, his back stooped and his steps slow, walked into the house. He looked up and gave a low whistle. "That's quite the ceiling."

Bridgette followed his gaze. The ceiling, repurposed from an old bank, was made of hammered metal tiles. "Glad you like it. Mom made Dad save it from a renovation he did years ago.

"Let me give you the tour, which I can do from right here." She pointed to a set of stairs, tucked behind the front door. "Those lead to the master suite. The door to the right goes to a second bedroom. The door on the left is a communication room. It's PI stuff, so don't ask too many questions. We do have a landline, but no cellular service. And this," she said, striding across the room and pulling open the drapes to a large window that overlooked the lake. The sun hung low in the afternoon sky.

"What a great view," said Luke. He stood right behind her, the heat from his body warming her skin. Why, then, was she covered in gooseflesh?

She remembered the last time they were at the lake together. It was the night before she left for college. They'd sat under the cottonwood tree and watched the sun set over the lake. As the sky darkened and the stars came out, their kisses grew more passionate. They'd had sex. It was a few moments that even now Bridgette recalled as painful and exhilarating. Funny, how she remembered the hitch in her breath as Luke entered her with a singular clarity. Yet, she couldn't recall the trip from the fishing cabin to her home later that night. As he kissed her good-night, they swore to keep in contact.

It was a promise neither of them kept beyond the first few months of the semester.

What would he say if he knew why she stopped keeping in touch?

Stripping a sheet from the chair, she said, "Give me a second to clear off the furniture and I'll get a fire started in the hearth."

"Point me in the direction of the woodpile and I can get the fire started," said Luke.

"It's behind the outbuilding," she said. "Just to the left of the back door."

As Luke left, Mr. Walker settled onto a bar stool at the kitchen counter. "This is a lovely place," he said.

Bridgette had spent her life being told she had access to lots of nice things. It always filled her with a mixture of pride and embarrassment, leaving her uncertain how to respond. It was true today, and she said, "I was told there was a big flood downtown, about twenty-two years ago."

"Oh, yeah," the older man said with a shake of his head. "It almost wiped Braxville off the map."

"Did you help with the cleanup, Mr. Walker?"

"Call me Paul. And, sure, I helped. My store was all but destroyed. Then again, there was me, owning the one hardware store in town. I was able to order a lot of what folks needed."

"What about the cleanup? Did you help?"

"Oh, yeah, everyone in town really pitched in." He paused. "Luke told me that there are a bunch of men who developed esophageal cancer. Do you think that there was something in those floodwaters that made us sick?"

"It's a possibility," she said, thankful that Luke had explained everything to his father beforehand.

"What other possibilities are there?" he asked.

"To be honest, Mr. Walker, that's why I'm here."

"Paul," he said again.

"An old habit dying hard, I guess," she said with a blush.

"What's this I hear about old habits?" Luke asked as he came into the house, his arms filled with firewood.

Her gaze followed as he passed, her middle filled with a fluttering. Luke was undeniably a handsome man. It was no wonder that they'd kissed last night or that he had been her first lover. Yet, there was more to him than a really nice bod. Luke Walker was a genuinely kind person.

"I was just trying to get Bridgette to call me Paul instead of Mr. Walker," said Luke's dad. "As hard as it is for you to call me Paul, it's harder for me to realize that both of you are grown-ups now."

"All right, Dad," said Luke, adding in a good-natured eye roll. Setting the stack of wood next to the hearth, he began to arrange sticks and logs.

Bridgette turned her attention back to Luke's father. "I have several questions to ask. They're all procedural. I'm trying to get an idea of your health history while looking for a link between you and all the other folks who are part of the cluster."

"Ask away," he said. "I'd be grateful for any information that you can give me."

As with all her cases, the weight of responsibility was heavy on Bridgette's shoulders. Yet, this case was different—it was too close to her home, literally. For one instant, she asked herself the unthinkable. What if more evidence surfaced that Colton Construction was involved? Could she really be impartial?

Chapter 13

Before leaving Braxville, Bridgette had started a file. She removed it from her bag and flipped it open. The first sheet was the health questionnaire she'd already mentioned. She got his height, weight and age before moving on to the rest of the items covered.

"Are you a smoker?" she began.

"No."

"Ever smoked?"

"Does trying twice when I was a teenager count?"

"Not really," said Bridgette, but it was her job to take note of everything.

"Prior to your cancer diagnosis, did you drink alcohol?"

"Sure."

"How often."

Paul puffed out his cheeks, blowing out the air in a single gust. "A beer or two a week."

"Any illegal drugs?"

"Never."

For the next thirty minutes, she asked questions about his health. As expected, there was nothing of note. Next, she moved on to his work history. Like the two generations of Walkers before Paul, he had helped his father run the hardware store. "I worked there six days a week from eighteen years old to the age of fifty-eight," Paul said, his chest expanding with pride.

"What changed when you turned fifty-eight?" Bridgette asked.

"He retired," said Luke. These were the first words he'd said in nearly half an hour. Once Luke had gotten the fire started and sat quietly in the adjacent living room.

"Why'd you retire at such a young age," Bridgette asked. Sure, it was an intrusive question, but intruding into all parts of Paul Walker's life was the only way to discover the truth.

"To be honest," said Paul, "I tire easily. It's hard to get through an entire day without needing a nap."

"Did you seek any medical opinion as to your lethargy?"

"The doctors ran a whole host of tests," said Luke, rising from the living room and coming to take a seat next to his father. "They checked for sleeping disorders, anemia, Lyme disease and found nothing wrong."

Paul added, "In the end, the doctor felt the cancer made me old before my time."

Bridgette couldn't help but think of Ernest O'Rourke and how he looked older than his years. Try as she might, Bridgette couldn't ignore the connection to Colton Construction. Despite the fact that she'd asked once before, she couldn't help but ask again. "And the only job you've ever held was at the hardware store?"

"The store is part of our family," he said with a sigh.

It was then that Bridgette noticed dark circles ringing Paul's eyes. His shoulders were stooped, and she figured now was the time he needed a rest. "Why don't you go to the sofa and enjoy the fire. I packed a cooler with sandwich fixings. It's in the SUV. We can eat before finishing the interview."

Opening the back door, Luke held it for Bridgette as she passed. "I'll help."

The sun was low on the horizon. The water of the lake reflected the sky, making it look as if there were two worlds, one stacked atop the other.

They returned to the cabin with the cooler. Stretched out, with his eyes closed, Luke's father snored softly.

"I didn't mean to wear him out," she said, a twinge of guilt in her chest.

"It's not you, but now you can see why he retired."

"He's lucky that you were able to take over the hardware store," said Bridgette.

Luke shrugged. "You know how it is with family-owned businesses."

She did. Sort of, at least.

"It's a nice time for a walk," said Luke. "Want to go while Dad naps?"

"Absolutely," said Bridgette as he grabbed a denim jacket and slipped it on.

Without discussion, thcy wandcrcd toward a trail through the woods. It was a path she knew well. Dried leaves carpeted the forest floor and crunched underfoot. "When I was a kid, my brothers and I pretended that elves and fairies lived in these woods and left out food. We were convinced elves took everything because it was always gone in the morning."

"Sounds like a nice childhood," said Luke.

"Ty and Jordana, being older and wiser, said we were dumb kids who didn't know better."

"Wow. That's harsh," he said.

"One night, I snuck out of the house to see what was taking the food we left."

"And what'd you find?" Luke asked.

"Raccoons," said Bridgette with a laugh.

They'd walked over half a mile, and there, in the middle of a clearing, was a well. The casing was green with moss and lichen. The stones were worn smooth from time and the weather. The crossbar was askew, and the only thing left from the rope was a few blackened strands. A wooden bench sat nearby, and Bridgette took a seat. "That night I kind of grew up. But to this day, I still think that this place is magical."

Dense woods encroached on the glade, the trees at the peak of their autumnal glory. Luke stood next to Bridgette, resting his foot on the bench's crossbeam. Her palms ached with the need to reach out and touch him. She slid her hands under her thighs.

He said, "I can see why you thought this place was magic, the raccoons notwithstanding."

She laughed. "You better watch out—I'm starting to like all your corny jokes."

"I'm not afraid, you know." He sat next to her, his thigh brushing against hers. "Should we talk about last night?" he asked.

"The kiss?" she asked, moving her leg closer to his.

"Yeah. The kiss. Was it just a kiss, or is there more?"

Bridgette had asked herself that same question more than once. She hadn't come up with an answer, which seemed to be an answer in itself. "I'm glad we've crossed paths again, Luke. You are a sincerely kind person."

"Uh-oh," he said. "Every good friend-zone speech begins with those exact words."

"I'm sorry," she said. "There's too much history between us, and I can't see repeating the same mistakes."

Luke's spine stiffened. He moved his leg and they no longer touched. "A mistake? Is that what I am to you—a freaking mistake?"

Damn. Bridgette's chest contracted.

Then memories of that day returned to her with a clarity that stole her breath. Bridgette was a freshman in college, just nineteen years old, and away from home for the first time in her life. She'd locked herself in one of the stalls of the communal bath and leaned against the metal wall. She stared at the plastic tube in her hand. A *plus* sign appeared in the results window of the pregnancy test.

She didn't need to read the directions. She knew what it meant. She was pregnant with Luke Walker's baby.

She had wrapped the pregnancy test in half a roll of toilet paper and shoved it deep into the garbage can by the door. Her eyes burned. Thank goodness that her roommate was in class. Bridgette couldn't have faced anyone else.

All the same, she couldn't suffer through the moment alone. She had to call, well, someone.

Her mother? Lilly was near to perfect and wouldn't understand how Bridgette—smart as she was—would make such a dumb mistake.

Jordana? Yvette? Sure, her sisters cared, but what could they have done?

Bridgette had known there was really only one person for her to call. Sliding up the face of her phone, she'd typed a series of numbers.

"Hey," said Luke, answering after the second ring. Her chest had hurt, making it hard to breathe. "Bridgette, is that you? Are you there?"

She'd wiped her eyes and put a smile in her voice. "Luke, how are you?"

"Lousy," he'd said. "I'm working, like constantly. You know my dad. He's not feeling too hot and can't work too much. I had to drop out of my intro to engineering class at the community college. This is total crap."

"I'm sorry, Luke. That does sound awful."

"It is." He had paused and huffed a breath. "What's worse, I'm actually worried. What if something's wrong with my dad again, you know?"

"I know," she said. In that moment, Bridgette had made a decision. She wouldn't burden Luke further.

"Did you call for a reason? Or just to chat?"

"Just to chat, I guess."

"Listen, I love the sound of your voice and I miss you, babe. A customer just came in. I gotta blow. Laters."

She never even got a chance to say goodbye. Before she could speak, the line was dead. Her stomach had contracted, bending her almost double. As the pain ebbed, Bridgette tried to tell herself that it was all a normal part of pregnancy.

Then again, she knew better.

Her period had started later that night.

And she had been left with a single question. *What if I had said something to Luke? Would things have turned out differently?*

Then she was back in the present. He was sitting beside her as the last light of day slipped beyond the horizon.

"Listen, Luke," she began. "I hadn't meant to imply that there's something wrong with you."

He looked over his shoulder, his eyes narrowed. "Did you hear that?"

"No," she said, following his gaze. "Hear what?"

"There's something in the bushes." Luke rose to his feet and walked toward a copse of trees with scrub clinging to the base of their trunks.

"Elves?" she joked. "Or is it a raccoon."

"It definitely sounded like someone walking through

the woods. Bigger than a raccoon and more real than an elf."

"This is all private property," said Bridgette. "Nobody else should be out here."

"Key word—*should.* Stay here," he said. "I'm going to check it out."

His sudden alarm left her heart racing. Bridgette stumbled after him. "You aren't going to leave me all by myself."

He paused and worked his jaw back and forth. Bridgette could tell that he wanted to argue. She didn't wait for what he planned to say, and she strode toward the tree line. Luke caught up with her. Grabbing her arm, he pulled back gently. "At least let me go first."

They walked into the woods. The spindly branches of trees rose to a sky of soft blue. Dried leaves covered the ground and crunched with each step taken. As the sun began to set, the air held a chill. "Maybe you just heard the wind in the trees," Bridgette suggested, even though she hadn't recalled a breeze blowing.

"Maybe," said Luke, his tone guarded.

"Well, whatever you heard is obviously gone now."

He turned a slow circle, scanning the forest. "I guess you're right. We should head back."

Side by side, Luke and Bridgette retraced their steps. Her earlier foible sat heavy on her chest. "You aren't a mistake," she said with an exhale. "There are just things that happened between you and me, things that make our past complicated. Do you understand?"

For a long moment, Luke said nothing. Then he grumbled, "Understand? Not at all."

"Can you trust me that we had complications and those scare the hell out of me?"

"Oh, so now I'm a complication?" His tone was as hard as flint.

"No, that's not what I meant, either." They'd returned to the clearing with the bench and the well. "We should just head back to the fishing cabin. If your dad wakes up, he'll wonder where we've gone."

Luke reached for her arm, pulling Bridgette to a stop. "Not a chance. It sounds like there's something important I need to know—and you haven't told me."

Bridgette shook her head and shrugged off his touch. "Forget I said anything."

"You've dropped more than one cryptic hint, Bridgette. Whatever the problem was, I have a right to know."

"The last time we were together at Lake Kanopolis," she began.

"The night before you went to college, you mean?"

"We, well, had sex."

"I remember that, too."

Bridgette couldn't find the right words. Then again there was nothing complicated about what she needed to say. "I got pregnant."

Luke went pale. "You what?"

"About two months after I went to college, I realized I was pregnant."

"Why in the hell is this the first time I'm hearing about a baby?"

"I called you," she began. "Your father was sick, forcing you to drop out of school. I couldn't add to your concerns. I decided to call you later and then…" Her voice caught with emotion. She shrugged.

"And then," Luke prodded.

"And then." Bridgette's eyes stung with unshed tears. She tried to blink them away, but they slipped down her cheeks. "I lost the baby and there was nothing more to tell."

Luke looked at the ground and shook his head. "I never knew."

"Of course not," said Bridgette, wiping away tears with the side of her sleeve. "I never told you."

"Have you ever told anyone? Or have you been living with this secret your entire life?"

She shrugged again.

"Your sisters?" he asked. "Your mom?"

With a shake of her head, she said, "No, none of them."

"You told your late husband, right?"

For the first time in her life, she realized telling Henry had been a betrayal of Luke. "I'm sorry. I just thought that after the miscarriage there was nothing else to concern you. I know now that I was wrong. I should have said something to you at some time."

Luke stepped toward Bridgette and wrapped his arms around her shoulders. He pulled her to him. She laid her head upon his chest and inhaled. His scent, the sweet smell of fresh-cut lumber and the musky scent of his skin, overwhelmed her senses. His hands rested on the small of her back. Her breasts were pressed against his pecs. To be held by Luke reminded Bridgette of how long she'd gone without the company of a man.

"I'm not mad," he said, his words washing over her.

Lifting her chin, Bridgette looked up at Luke. "What are you, then?"

"Sad, I guess. I wish things would've worked out differently."

In the days and weeks to come, Bridgette wasn't sure how the kiss began. Had she placed her mouth on Luke's first? Or was it the other way around? What she did know was that their lips were pressed together, their tongues in a tangled dance.

He gripped her breast, rubbing his thumb over her nipple. Despite her layers of clothes, she hardened under his touch.

"Oh, Luke," she moaned.

He placed a line of kisses on her throat and she began to burn from within. Desire consumed her. She splayed her hands across his chest, his heartbeat racing beneath her palms. Bridgette reached for the hem of his shirt and pulled it up, exposing a line of his abdomen. She ran her fingers over his flesh.

He gripped her ass, pressing her to him. He was hard and wanted her as much as she wanted him. She lowered her touch, feeling his length through the fabric of his jeans. He let out a low growl.

"You like when I touch you like that?" she asked, nipping his bottom lip with her teeth.

"God, yes," he breathed.

She worked the buttons of his fly loose and reached into his jeans, stroking the silky skin of his sex. It had been so long since she'd touched anyone in an intimate way. For a moment, Bridgette wondered if she'd forgotten how to give—or receive—pleasure. A bead of moisture clung to the head of his penis. She collected it with the tip of her finger and glided her palm down his shaft.

He claimed her mouth with his, and this time the kiss was hard and urgent. "God, you're so sexy and that feels fantastic," he said, grabbing a handful of her hair. "But I want to make you feel good, too."

"I can wait my turn," she said.

"Or we can do this together."

"Out here? In the woods?" She worked her hand up and down his length, and Luke hardened with her touch.

"Who's here to see us?" he asked, unfastening the top button of her pants. He pulled down the zipper and reached into her jeans and then her panties.

Bridgette was already wet, and he slid his finger over the opening of her sex. His touch sent a shock wave of pleasure through her body, and she trembled with desire. "Do you like it when I touch you like that?" he asked, echoing her earlier question.

"Yes," she said. She parted her thighs, giving Luke more access. Bridgette could feel herself slipping away and expanding at the same time. She was becoming one with a feeling as old as time, while experiencing something that was wholly new.

The climax crashed down on Bridgette with the force of an avalanche and left her breathless. How long had it been since a hand other than her own had brought her pleasure? Then again, she knew the answer.

The last time she had been touched was two years ago. For the first time, she no longer needed to cling to the past. The question was—what did Bridgette want to find in her future?

Chapter 14

Luke wanted one thing in the world—to make love to Bridgette Colton. He slipped his finger inside of her. Her muscles clenched and pulsed as the last of the climax rippled through her body. She continued to touch him, working her hand up and down his shaft. The pleasure was exquisite, yet it wasn't enough to satisfy his need.

"I want you," he said, his mouth on hers. "Tell me you want me, too."

"I want you, Luke. I want you inside of me so bad."

It was all the invitation he needed. From his wallet, he took out a condom. Then Luke pulled down his pants, just enough to free himself. As he rolled on the condom, Bridgette kicked off one shoe and stripped out of one leg of her pants.

He sat on the bench. She sank down on Luke, taking him in one stroke. His nuts tightened, warning Luke that he was ready to climax. That wouldn't do. He wanted to take his time with Bridgette, to savor the moment as she rode him.

Long and slow, she moved down and back up, until just his tip was inside of her. Luke looked to where their bodies met and became one. The tightening in his balls was an excruciating bliss.

Wrapping his hand through her hair, Luke pulled back on her head, exposing her neck and bringing up her breasts. He kissed the skin of her throat while working his hand into her shirt, her bra. He twisted each nipple between his finger and thumb and smiled as she moaned with pleasure. Her strokes became faster, more frantic. Her breathing came in short gasps.

Luke lifted her shirt, exposing her breasts. He took one of Bridgette's nipples in his mouth, rolling it with his tongue. She cried out as she came, and Luke could hold on no longer. A prickling began at the back of his neck, traveling down his spine. It ended with his climax, which came hard and fast. As his pulse slowed and the sweat from his brow dried, Luke gently kissed Bridgette's lips.

"That was magnificent," he said. "You were magnificent."

"You aren't so bad yourself," said Bridgette, nuzzling his neck. "I'd forgotten how good this could be."

Sure, he wondered if Bridgette meant sex in general or, specifically, making love to him. But he knew enough to not ask, to just appreciate the compliment—and the way she fitted perfectly in his arms.

He wound his fingers through hers. "I'm glad we found each other again," he said. "And that you're back home."

"It's just while I complete this investigation. Then I'll go back to Wichita."

Luke had a bad feeling about where Bridgette's head—and heart—might be as far as he was concerned. He swore, if only to himself, that he'd give her all the space she needed and not push for anything more than this moment.

Bridgette wiggled off his lap and sat on the bench. Slipping into her pants, she refastened her jeans and put on her shoe. Retying the laces, she said, "I can't make any promises to you about the future. All I can offer you is the next few weeks, and if that's not enough, well, then..." She let her words unravel the thread that tied his heartstrings together.

"I understand," said Luke, a throbbing in his chest. Hadn't he known from the beginning that any connection with Bridgette was fleeting? Being with her was like holding sand in his grip. The tighter he squeezed, the more of her slipped away.

All the same, he had hoped for a different answer. More than that, he thought the news of the pregnancy lost had brought them closer. Now it seemed as if Bridgette was less accessible than ever.

Then again, he had other more immediate problems. Like what to do with the used condom? Thank goodness he had a few crumpled napkins in his jeans pocket and a plastic bag from the store in his jacket.

Bridgette turned away and gave Luke a moment of privacy while he got cleaned up. Luke stood and shoved the plastic bag deep into the back pocket of his jeans. He'd throw the whole mess away once he got a minute.

Maybe his thoughts about Bridgette were too harsh. Before making love, he hadn't asked for any promises—and she hadn't given any.

The sky was orange, with pink at the edges. Soon it would be full dark. "We better head back. I'm sure my dad's awake by now."

"And he's worried about us?" Bridgette offered.

They walked away from the bench and the well, their fingers were close but not touching. Luke dared not take Bridgette's hand in his own although he wanted to all the same.

"Dad, worried?" Luke echoed with a chuckle. "I doubt it. I think he's helped himself to the food you brought, and we might not have much left for our own sandwiches by the time we get back."

Bridgette folded her arms over her chest and gave a small laugh, as well.

"Cold?" he asked.

"A little," she said. Luke slipped out of his coat and draped the jacket over her shoulders. "Thanks," she said with a smile.

Luke looked away. There, in the distance, he saw the glint of a light. He stopped. "What's over there?" he asked.

"The woods," said Bridgette.

"No houses? No neighbors?"

"No. The Coltons own acres of this land."

Luke went cold and it wasn't from the chilly night air. He jogged toward the light. Then, unmistakable in the silence of the woods, was the sound of a car's engine revving.

Julia stared through the ocular lens—the binoculars trained on Luke. His lips were pressed together. He scanned the woods. She would have sworn he was too far away to hear when she started the engine.

She'd been wrong.

Dropping her foot on the accelerator, she pulled hard on the steering wheel. The car jostled over the rutted track as the wheels dipped over the lip of a ravine. She slammed her foot on the brake and jerked the gearshift into Reverse. Slowly the car inched backward. She put the auto in Drive and turned the car back toward the road. With the grille finally facing forward, she sped down the bumpy track that wound through the woods. The front fender of her car rose as she crested a hill. For a moment, Julia was suspended in the air, and then the tires slammed down. Julia hit the seat and her teeth cracked.

She pressed her foot onto the accelerator harder. The undercarriage of her car mowed down a small tree. The engine whined as the car shimmied.

Dammit.

Dammit.

Dammit.

What had she broken now? Or maybe the question

she should be asking was whether the car was able to get away.

The track leveled off and the shaking stopped. The squealing engine quieted at least a little.

Last night she had told the police officer that she'd never bother Luke or Bridgette again. Certainly, following them to the lake, trespassing while spying on them in the most intimate moment, would be considered bothering.

What did that mean for her? Would the police be waiting when she got home?

Would Julia be sent back to the hospital? Or worse, jail?

The forest thinned and the track widened. Her headlights caught an opening in the tree line and, beyond that, a sliver of road. Turning onto the blacktop, Julia knew that she was out of the woods, at least in the literal sense.

Yet, there would be consequences—horrible costs—for what she had done.

As she drove, her pulse slowed. As the road stretched out like a long, gray ribbon, her mind wandered. She'd been horrified and fascinated as Luke had made love to Bridgette Colton. Lips. Arms. Legs. All tangled together.

In the moment, Julia tried to look away—really, she had. In the end, she was helpless to do anything other than watch.

The sight had sent her pulse racing. As she drove, Julia knew that she'd felt more than lust at the sight; there was rage, as well. The anger began to smolder until it was the white heat of a flame, and Julia knew that someone was about to get burned.

Sprinting through the forest, Luke hurtled over a felled tree. His toe caught the decaying wood, breaking it into a thousand splinters. Ducking under a low branch, he pressed forward. Thorny bushes reached out, scratching his face and hands as he ran.

He didn't care.

Someone had been in the woods. He wasn't going to let them escape.

Behind, he heard Bridgette's labored breathing as she struggled to keep up. He pushed his legs to go faster, determined to place himself between her and whatever danger might lie ahead.

The path the car had taken was easy to follow. The tires chewed up the undergrowth and had mowed down dozens of small trees and bushes. He ran up an incline and skidded to a stop. There, in the dying light, lay a dented hubcap.

Bridgette came up a moment later. Gripping her knees, she bent over to catch her breath. "Who was it? Did you see the car?"

With a shake of his head, Luke said, "They're gone now." Sidestepping to the bottom of the hill, he picked up the metal disk. It told him nothing, yet he held it up for Bridgette to see. Continuing, he said, "But whoever it is, they lost this."

Starting up the hill, something else caught his attention. Dropping to a knee, he ran a finger over the damp dirt. Luke rubbed a finger with his thumb. The scent and viscosity were unmistakable. "Motor oil."

"My guess," said Bridgette, from her spot atop the hill. "The car came over this ridge and landed hard. It lost the hubcap and cracked something in the undercarriage." Luke gaped and said nothing. She added, "Remember, I grew up around a lot of construction sites. And, I am an investigator."

Unable to hold back his smile, Luke said, "I guess you are both. Now let's get out of here. I don't think whoever it was is coming back, but I don't want to hang around and find out if they do."

"Whoever?" asked Bridgette. Luke reached the top of the ridge. "You don't think your ex-girlfriend was spying on us again?"

Luke couldn't lie to Bridgette. "It could be a random person, but I doubt it was anyone other than Julia."

"Which means she saw us while we, well, you know...."

Luke clenched his teeth together. "I should have showed more restraint, Bridgette. I'm sorry that you were put into that situation."

"It's not like you were alone or I didn't have some kind of say in the matter."

"So, you aren't mad?"

"At you?" she asked. Shaking her head, she continued. "Not at all. I am furious with Julia. She's gone too far this time."

Luke said, "I'll call Reese. It'll be easy to see if Julia is missing this hubcap."

"You'll have to wait until we get back to town.

There's no cellular coverage at the fishing cabin. Mom's rules, so we can all unplug and connect."

Luke glanced at his phone. "I have three bars," he said.

"Are you joking?" Bridgette asked, looking at his screen. "That's weird. Just don't tell Mom."

He actuated the speaker function before placing the call. Reese answered. "Luke, what's up?"

"It's Julia again." Luke took a few minutes explaining what had happened with the car on the private road, along with the suspicion that it had been Julia. "I found a hubcap," Luke said. "Can you check and see if she's home, and if her wheel's been damaged."

"I'm on it," said Reese. "Did anyone get hurt?"

"Spooked is all," said Luke, leaving out any intimate details of what Julia might've seen.

"I'll get back to you after paying Julia a second visit," said Reese.

"And then what?" Bridgette asked.

"If her car's missing a hubcap, I'll bring her in to the station. If we can prove that it came from her vehicle, she'll be charged with trespassing, vandalism, and several other minor crimes. Hopefully, it's enough to convince your ex that she needs to end her obsession."

"I appreciate anything you can do," said Luke, ending the call. Then to Bridgette, he said, "Now, we have to let the police do their job." He paused. "Speaking of jobs, did you learn anything from my father?"

Luke and Bridgette retraced their steps. The sky was a deep shade of violet, and lights from the Colton fishing cabin shone through the dark.

"Do you remember anything about a flood when we were kids?"

"Sure," he said. "We were in grade school when it happened. I remember helping my dad with one job or another—gutting buildings, hauling away debris."

"It seems like a lot of people were involved in the cleanup, including several of the other victims. With all the older buildings downtown, it's possible that carcinogens were released into the floodwaters."

"It makes sense."

Bridgette nodded. "And yet, there's something I don't like about that theory. You just said that you were part of a cleanup crew, but you're healthy. If there was something caustic in the water—say arsenic that was used as a wallpaper base—why are there only half a dozen cases from decades ago? I'd expect to see hundreds." She continued, "And it does nothing to explain why there are men who weren't around for the flood and are now getting sick."

Luke didn't have an answer for either of her questions. As they approached the house, his father opened the door. "There you are. When I woke up, you were gone."

"We just went for a walk," said Luke, not willing to share much more with his father.

"What's that you have in your hands?" he asked. "Is that a hubcap?"

Luke opened the rear liftgate and threw the metal disk into his father's SUV. "Just something we picked up in the woods."

"Well, come on in," said Luke's dad. "I saw the sandwich fixings and have nice enough manners to wait for you all."

Bridgette laughed. "Luke said that you'd have eaten everything before we got back."

"Really?" Luke asked with mock indignation. "You're going to throw me under the bus?"

"I'll admit to snacking a little," said Luke's father. "But now that you're here, let's get some food."

Within minutes, everything for a meal had been set on the counter. While throwing away the bag with the condom and cleaning up, Luke took a few moments to think. He'd only been gone from the fishing cabin for an hour—and yet everything had changed.

He'd made love to Bridgette Colton. And there was no denying his feelings to himself—he had come to care for her once again. No, that wasn't true. He'd always cared about her. Yet, did sex mean they had a future together?

Years ago they had created a life. Despite the fact that the pregnancy had ended, Luke liked the idea of Bridgette being the mother to his children.

And then there were other concerns that were far less pleasant.

His ex-girlfriend was more determined than he had ever imagined. Moreover, Bridgette was obviously the target of Julia's wrath.

It meant that Bridgette was in danger, not just now, but until she left Braxville.

Chapter 15

Dinner at the lake house, cleanup and the ride back to Braxville were all uneventful—something that brought Bridgette a great deal of gratitude. Life had been more problematic than ever since returning home. Now Bridgette had to parse out her feelings for Luke.

No, that wasn't true.

She knew how she felt.

What she didn't know was if she wanted to act on those feelings? First, she'd lost a child and then a husband. Was Bridgette ready to try for love again?

At least she had more anecdotal evidence that the cancer had been caused by something in the flood waters. True, there were holes in her theory, but for the moment it was the most solid one that she had.

Since Paul Walker had only worked at the hardware

store, he couldn't have been an employee of Colton Construction. It meant that her family's business was in no way connected to the cluster.

She was more relieved about that fact than she cared to admit.

As he had done before, Luke drove his father's SUV. He returned to Main Street, and from there, Paul would drive himself home.

Bridgette opened the door and slipped out of the large auto. Luke and his father did the same, and they all stood near the grille of the SUV, headlights illuminating the empty road.

Wind swirled around the corner, creating a dust devil of leaves and debris. Bridgette shivered with the cold. "Thank you for taking the time to meet with me," she said. "You've been very helpful."

Paul said, "Getting cancer changed my life. In some ways, I'm a better man because of everything I went through. I appreciate my family and friends more. I look at every day as a gift. But the illness has taken a physical toll." With a shake of his head, he continued, "If you can figure out what caused me to get sick, I'd surely appreciate it."

"I promised your son that I would do just that," she said.

"Well, you kids have a nice evening. Luke, I'll be in touch." As Paul rounded to the driver's side and opened the door, he said, "And, Bridgette, tell your dad I said hello. I kind of miss old Fitz. He used to come by the hardware store back when the construction company wasn't as big as it is now." Before she could comment,

Paul continued, "And then there was the time when they renovated the mall downtown. Business was slow at the store, so I worked for your dad on that job. A good man but a hard boss."

Bridgette could not recall getting from the street to Luke's apartment. When she finally became aware of her senses, she stood in the middle of his living room. The light from several lamps filled the room. Her head throbbed with each beat of her heart. She was deaf to every sound beyond her rushing pulse and her own breath.

"What's the matter?" Luke asked. He had ahold of her arm and led her to the sofa, where he gently guided her to sitting. "Should I call someone? Your mom? One of your sisters? A doctor?"

His touch was warm. His hand was strong. She said nothing.

"You okay?" he asked.

Bridgette was far from okay. "Can you turn off one of the lamps?" she asked. "It's too bright in here."

Luke flipped a switch by the door. Two of the lights went dark. "Better?" he asked.

"Much."

"So," he began, taking a seat next to her. "What happened?"

Leaning her head back on the sofa, Bridgette pinched the bridge of her nose. "To be honest, I don't know."

"You were talking to my dad and you turned pale. You were able to walk, when I led you up the stairs. But as the old saying goes, the lights were on, but nobody was home."

"That about sums it up, I guess." Bridgette tried to laugh, but there was nothing funny about her situation. The sound came out as a snort.

"Let me get you a glass of water."

Luke filled a glass with water from the tap. Returning, he set the glass on the coffee table. "Drink," he said.

She lifted the cup with a hand that trembled. Water sloshed over the rim and soaked into the sleeve of her sweater. After taking a sip, she set the glass down. "Better," she said. "Thanks."

"Can you tell me what happened out there now? I still think I should call someone," he said, reaching inside his jacket for his phone.

"Don't," she said, her hand on his wrist. "Your father told me something that was… Oh, I don't know."

"Was it upsetting?" Luke offered.

"I'm not sure what to call how I feel. What's the word for upsetting times a thousand? He gave a bit of information that proves a supposition about the cancer clusters."

"Does it have to do with the flood?"

"No," said Bridgette with a shake of her head.

"What is it then?"

Before she could decide what to share or not, her phone rang. She fished it from her pocket and glanced at the screen. It was her coworker, Rachel. "I have to take this," she said to Luke, while swiping the call open.

"Rachel, what's up?"

"I wanted you to know, I've gotten one of the disks open."

"And?" Bridgette's heart hammered against her chest.

"It looks like the data is password protected. Until we can get around that, we won't be able to access any of the information. I like to think that I can do everything on a computer, but right now I'm stumped." She paused. "My recommendation is that we send the disks to the state IT department. They have tech I don't have at the office."

"You only need a password?" Bridgette asked.

"Finding the right code is a lot harder than *only*."

"I'm on my way," Bridgette said.

"What are you going to be able to do?"

"My mother set up the disks. I might be able to figure out what password she used."

"I'll see you soon."

Bridgette ended the call and rose to her feet. Like she was suddenly standing on the deck of a ship in the middle of a storm, the room seemed to pitch to the side. Her vision darkened at the edges. Luke's strong hand gripped her arm.

"I'm not asking if you're okay again. Obviously, you aren't." He pulled her toward the sofa. "Sit back down."

The floor leveled and Bridgette inhaled, her vision clearing. "I need to go to my office," she said.

"Tonight?"

"Right now."

"I'm not letting you leave until we know what's going on. Your health is more important than your job, Bridgette."

"This from a man who does nothing but work," she said, trying to pull her arm from his grasp. It didn't work.

"If you can make a joke, then I guess you are feeling

a bit better." Luke's grip loosened, but he didn't let go. "Then again, I know how you'll be safe."

"How's that?" she asked.

"I'm going to go with you."

Bridgette didn't have time to argue with him, especially since she suspected that she was suffering from shock. Being escorted by a capable friend made sense.

"All right," she said, acquiescing to his demand. "Let's go."

Luke held Bridgette's arm as they walked down the flight of stairs. Outside, a cool breeze blew droplets of rain. The wind and the water revived her, at least a little, and her thinking cleared.

"My truck is parked behind the store," said Luke. "Let's get it and I'll drive you."

"My office is only a few blocks away. Besides, the walk will do me some good."

"Are you finally going to tell me what's going on?"

"At the very beginning of the investigation, I had a suspicion," she said, walking down the street. "Several of the men who got sick used to work for my father's company. Then the investigative team learned about the flood, and in a way being exposed to carcinogens in dirty water makes perfect sense."

"But then my father mentioned that he worked for Colton Construction," said Luke.

"Moreover, three men from the original cancer cluster not only worked for my dad but on the renovation of the downtown mall, as well."

"And you were kind of traumatized once you put all of those pieces together," said Luke.

"I was able to get all employee information from my mother, who used to be the office manager. The tech was pretty old, so it's taken some time to get the disks open."

"There could be other things that connect all the men in the cluster beyond Colton Construction."

"Thanks for trying to make me feel better," she said as they approached City Hall. At this time of the night the building was locked, and Bridgette swiped her ID over a sensor. The latch clicked and she shouldered the door open. Automatic lights switched on as they walked down the corridor, illuminating their way.

Her office was on the second floor. The door was unlocked, and she walked in. The old boxy computer still filled the conference table. Rachel wore her hair in a ponytail and sat in front of a monitor. Looking up as Bridgette walked in, she gave a wan smile. "That was quick," she said.

"I'm renting an apartment a few blocks away for now." Stepping aside so Luke could enter the small work space, Bridgette continued, "This is Luke Walker." She paused, not entirely sure how to categorize their relationship. "A friend."

"I know you," said Rachel, getting out of the chair and giving Luke a wide smile. "You own the hardware store downtown."

"I do."

Was Rachel flirting with Luke? A hot flash of anger and jealousy sprang up in Bridgette's chest. She immediately tamped it down. She had more pressing worries than her love life.

As she slipped into the seat just vacated by her coworker, Bridgette's mouth went dry. Was she really about to do this? The screen was gray, with silver lettering. The cursor blinked in a field of lighter gray. Password.

"The key is six characters. It can be numbers, letters, a combination," she said. "Don't worry about locking yourself out. I was able to override that part of the system."

"For my mom," said Bridgette. "Six characters means a date. I'm going to start with the most obvious one first," she continued while typing. "My parents' anniversary."

Six dots appeared, shimmied and disappeared.

Incorrect password.

"My dad's birthday," Bridgette said, entering the date.

Incorrect password.

She tried her mother's birthday, and the birthday of Bridgette and each of her siblings.

The message, *incorrect password*, flashed on the screen again and again.

"Try Colton," Luke said. "That has six letters."

"Good suggestion," said Rachel.

Bridgette turned back to the screen and typed.

Incorrect password.

She used all capital letters. All lowercase letters.

Nothing worked.

"It could be random. Or another word. Maybe the name of one of your siblings. Or a pet," said Rachel.

"There are a few things I know about my mother,"

said Bridgette. Lacing her fingers behind her head, she stared at the computer. "The password won't be random, and it'll be related to family. I don't think she'd use a name of one of the kids because she'd feel guilty about the five others who she didn't pick." It gave her an idea and she typed *T-J-B-N-B-Y.* "The first letter for everyone's name," she said, hitting the enter key.

Incorrect password.

"Can you think of anything else?" Luke asked. He leaned forward, his arm grazing her shoulder. An electric charge ran up Bridgette's arm.

"No," she began. "I have one last idea," she said, typing out six numbers. It was the birthdate for her uncle, Shep. "Let's see if it'll work."

The password field disappeared, and for a moment the screen went black.

"What happened?" Bridgette asked. "Did I do something wrong?"

"I don't know," said Rachel. "I'm not used to this operating system. Maybe my override wasn't as secure as I thought."

Then rows of text scrolled up the screen.

"I think we're in," said Rachel.

Bridgette's hands were cold and damp. She pressed her palms into her thighs to keep them from trembling. The text stopped scrolling and a menu of documents filled the screen. She opened one titled Employee Contact Information. There was a list of names, along with dates of employment. Bridgette found the ones she expected to see. Ernest O'Rourke, the foreman. His buddies—Tom Cromwell, Bill Warner. Paul Walker was on the list, having worked for Colton Construction during the mall renovation. Bridgette glanced at the whiteboard and the list of men who were part of the cancer cluster.

One by one, she found them on the official list of past employees.

"Do you know what this means?" Rachel asked.

Bridgette did know and all too well. "Colton Construction is definitely the point of contact for everyone who got sick."

Julia had no place to go, no safe place to stay. She knew with every beat of her racing heart that Luke had called the police. The cops would be waiting at her home, ready to cart her off to jail.

What would she say?

How could she defend against what she'd done?

She'd die before being locked up again.

If that were the case, why couldn't she leave Luke alone?

She drove, without destination, as images from the woods played over and over in her mind. This time, it was Julia who straddled Luke.

Why hadn't he made love to Julia? Or even kissed her for that matter? Did he think she was too pure?

Luke was her soul mate. They were destined to be together. Julia had to make him see that truth.

But how?

A sensor sounded.

Ding. Ding. Ding.

Damn. The gas gauge leaned lethargically to the side. Empty. Julia knew that the time had come, and she turned for home. Maneuvering the car onto her street, she held her breath. Where Julia expected to see a police cruiser, there was nothing.

Pulling into the driveway, she turned off the ignition and stepped from the car. Her eyes burned from staring at the road, and her hands ached from gripping the steering wheel. She stood and her knees creaked like the hinges of a long-neglected door. She hobbled up the walkway, not sure why her house looked different. She tried to put the key into the lock, and the teeth scraped against metal.

Why hadn't her mother turned on the lights? Was something wrong with Momma?

Her pulse began to hammer against her ribs as a million awful thoughts filled her mind at once. She fumbled with the key, dropped it. With a curse, she knelt on the darkened concrete and blindly groped for the key.

Her fingers brushed against the cold metal. She stood and tried once more. This time, the key slid home and she turned the handle, opening the door.

The TV in the living room was dark. A single light, above the stove, blazed in the kitchen. No savory aromas wafted through the house.

"Momma?" Julia called out.

Nothing.

The house was dark and cold as a tomb.

"Momma?" she said, louder this time.

Nothing.

Rushing to her mother's bedroom, Julia opened the door and flipped on the overhead light. The bed was made. A set of pajamas was laid out across the pillows.

Tears stung Julia's eyes as she rushed to the adjacent bathroom.

Empty.

The hall bath was empty, as well.

In each room, Julia turned on lights, calling out her single word. "Momma?"

"Momma?"

"Momma?"

The metallic taste of panic coated her tongue. Her legs were heavy, her arms were limp.

She couldn't fall apart, not when her mother needed her. What Julia had to do was think. Dammit, think.

What facts did she know? Her mother wasn't home. Her mother couldn't drive. She didn't visit neighbors. Aside from Julia, Momma really didn't have much except church on Sunday.

Had the ladies from church stopped by to collect Julia's mother? Was she right now in the church hall, eating cookies and drinking punch? If that was the case, why hadn't her mother left a note?

Maybe the plans had been made earlier? Had Momma told Julia, who then had forgotten?

There was nothing to be done beyond go to church and check for herself.

She strode toward the door. Passing the hall bath, Julia caught a glimpse of herself in the mirror.

Mud was smeared across her cheek. A dried leaf clung to her hair. There was a stain on her rumpled shirt, along with a rip on the knee of her pants from a tumble that Julia didn't recall taking. She needed to find her mother, but first she'd get cleaned up and change.

Pivoting, she raced to her room. Pushing the door open, Julia stopped on the threshold and sucked in a breath.

There, sitting in her wheelchair, was her mother.

"Momma, there you are. Thank goodness you're okay."

Nothing.

"Did you hear me calling for you? I was really worried that something bad had happened to you."

Nothing.

Her mother worked her jaws back and forth. Her eyes were red rimmed and watery. It was then that Julia noticed other details.

First, her walls were stripped bare.

Every picture of Luke was gone. The tickets from the movie they'd seen had disappeared. The napkins were gone.

Julia's small metal wastepaper basket sat in front of her mother. In one of her mother's hands was a bottle of rubbing alcohol. In the other, a box of matches.

"You promised to leave Luke Walker alone," her mother said.

"I did," said Julia, stepping forward and peering into the garbage can. Every bit of the shrine she'd built was inside. "I have."

"That nice policeman stopped by today," her mother said. The temperature in the room seemed to plummet and Julia began to shiver.

"What'd he say?" she asked, her voice shaking.

"He wanted to know where you were. He was wondering because someone was trespassing out by the Coltons' fishing cabin today."

"I can explain, Momma," she began.

"I'm done with your lies." With a shake of her head, Julia's mother dumped the entire bottle of rubbing alcohol into the waste basket. She struck a match, the scent of sulfur dioxide hung in the air. Her mother let go of the lit match. It tumbled end over end, the flames blue and orange, until it landed in the can.

Whoosh. Flames consumed every memory, every moment spent with Luke.

"Mother," Julia screamed. "What have you done?"

"I'm giving you a clean slate," said her mother. "You need to get over this obsession. You're clinging to a relationship that isn't rooted in reality. It's just like before, but I'm not going to let you go on any longer."

Julia reached for the can. The metal was hot and burned her skin. She screamed, jerking her hand back and tipping the can over. Sparks struck her mother's pants. The cloth immediately caught fire.

"Julia," her mother yelled. "Help me."

She lunged forward, ready to grab a blanket and smother out the flames.

Then she stopped.

"Why should I?" Julia asked, her jaw tight. "You were the one who started the fire. Now, you can burn in hell."

Chapter 16

Cold wind whipped around the corner. Bridgette wished she'd worn something warmer than a sweater and jeans. Folding her arms across her chest, she walked faster, wanting nothing more than a hot cup of tea and a night in her own bed.

"Penny for your thoughts?" Luke asked, opening the door that led to the apartments above the hardware store.

"I need about a million dollars' worth of answers," she said. "I can't ignore the connection between Colton Construction and the cancer cases. But what I don't know is what I need to do next."

"We," he said. "What we need to do next."

They'd reached the landing and stood between the

two doors. "This is my job and my responsibility," she said. "It's my family. I have to take care of the problem."

Luke nodded, although she wasn't sure that he was agreeing or simply acquiescing.

Bridgette continued, "I just don't know how."

"This can't be the first time you've found a connection between a business and an illness."

"It's not," she said. They were inside. The wind no longer blew, yet Bridgette still shivered and her voice trembled.

"What did you do then?" he asked.

She hesitated a moment, drawing in her arms closer to her chest. "I closed down the business. It's a matter of public safety."

He said nothing. Then again, what was there to say?

"I should go," she said at length, turning for the door to the apartment she had rented.

Reaching for her hand, Luke pulled her to a stop. "The window hasn't been fixed yet," he said. "And we have every reason to believe that Julia was spying on us in the woods."

"I know what you're implying, that I can't stay alone," she said. "Don't worry about me. I'll be fine."

Luke shook his head. "Fine isn't good enough for me."

He still held her hand. His flesh was warm. His grip was strong. She recalled the feel of his palms as they had skimmed her body. His mouth on hers. The waves of pleasure that moved through her body as she came.

"I'm a big girl," she said, letting her fingers slip through his grip.

"I know just what kind of girl you are," he said, stepping toward her. "I know you are capable, smart—and sexy as hell. But here, in my house, it's my job to protect you."

Bridgette swallowed, trying to think of something to say. She was saved by the trilling of Luke's cell phone. He removed the phone from his pocket and glanced at the screen. Brows drawn together, he swiped the call open. "Yes?"

Bridgette was less than a foot away from Luke. In the small space she could hear everything the caller said. "This is Nancy, Julia's mother."

"Why are you calling from the hospital?" he asked. "Is everything okay?"

"There was an accident—and a fire," the woman said. To Bridgette, the older woman sounded weary and worried.

"Did Julia have anything to do with either?" Luke asked.

"Just tell me," said the woman. "Have you seen her? Has she tried to contact you?"

To Bridgette, the non-answer was answer enough. What had Julia done to her mother?

Nancy continued, "I just want to know that she's safe."

"If I see her at all," said Luke. "I'll call Detective Carpenter. But what about you?"

"The doctors are taking care of me now. I'll be spending the next few nights with a friend from church." Julia's mother paused. "My daughter's not a bad person. She just gets these ideas and can't let them go, that's all."

"I'll call if I see or hear anything," said Luke, and he ended the call. Then to Bridgette he said, "That was Julia's mother."

"I heard everything."

"I know you want to be independent. I also know that I'm not letting you stay by yourself, not with Julia out there—" he gestured to the locked door at the bottom of the stairs "—somewhere."

Bridgette shook her head. "Running to someone who can keep me safe feels like giving up. Then it means that Julia has disrupted my life and won."

"If she hurts you," he said, "she's won as well." He opened the door to his apartment. "Let's finish this conversation inside."

When was the last time someone had cared about her well-being, much less insisted that they keep her safe? "I'm sure the police will find Julia soon. But I'll stay with you tonight."

"With me?" he asked, his voice low as they crossed the threshold and Luke closed the door behind them.

Bridgette had meant that she'd sleep on the sofa. But the frantic sex in the woods hadn't sated her desires as she hoped. In fact, taking Luke as a lover had awakened longings that Bridgette had tried to bury with her late husband.

"Would that be so bad?" she asked, casting a glance at the window. The shades had already been drawn and there was no chance that they might be seen from the street below. Continuing, she reached for his hand and ran a finger over his wrist. "Would you mind terribly?"

Whatever she was about to say next was cut short.

Luke reached for Bridgette, pulling her to him. Her breasts were pressed against his chest. She wrapped her arms around his neck, running her fingers through his hair and pulling him closer.

He was already hard, and her pulse began to race.

She wanted—no, needed—Luke inside her.

Bridgette splayed her hands across his chest. His heartbeat resonated under her palms. She rocked her hips forward, savoring the feel of his length. She wasn't so stupid as to think that having sex for a second time in a single day wouldn't deepen their relationship. And Bridgette didn't know what she wanted from Luke, or life—beyond the moment.

Was it fair to him—and to her?

Did she care?

His mouth moved to her throat. His kisses were hot and ignited a fire inside of her. Bridgette moaned.

Luke claimed her mouth with his. She closed her eyes and let the kiss take away all her worries.

His touch was no longer making up for time lost or regret for the past. Now it was all about dominance and surrender.

Luke lifted Bridgette's shirt, exposing her flesh, and brought it over her breasts. He bent his head to her chest, running his tongue between her cleavage. He pulled one breast free from her bra's cup and scraped his teeth over her nipple.

The sensation sent a shock wave of pain and pleasure rippling through Bridgette. She looked down to her own body. Her skin was slick and wet. Her nipple was pink and hard. Luke's tongue swept over her breast and Bridgette's knees went weak with desire.

"Take me," she said.

Flicking his tongue over her breast once more, Luke smiled. "I will, just not now."3 As he spoke, he worked his fingers down the front of her pants and into her panties. A second finger joined the first, and she opened herself up to take him in all the way. He continued, his blue eyes locked with hers. "Earlier, we were rushed. Now, I intend to take my time."

Time? Bridgette felt as if she were a ticking bomb, and without Luke she might explode. He continued to work his fingers inside of her, her muscles clenched as he rubbed the top of her sex. Her climax came quickly and left her breathless. She clung to his shoulders as her heartbeat slowed.

"Kiss me," she whispered.

He placed his mouth on hers as he slipped his hands from her pants. He painted Bridgette's lips, still wet with her musk.

Bridgette circled her tongue around one finger and then the other. She took him in her mouth and sucked. He growled with pleasure.

His gaze met hers, and Bridgette's heart began to thunder in her chest. Luke kissed her once more before tugging on the hem of her shirt and pulling it over her head. He opened the clasp on her bra. The straps slid down her arms and the undergarment dropped to the floor. It landed on top of her shirt. With his lips pressed to her lobe, he whispered, "Take off your pants."

His words danced along her skin until gooseflesh

covered her skin, his eyes so intense she could do nothing beyond obey. She stripped until clad only in her panties.

Bridgette wasn't embarrassed by her body. Sure, she could spend a few more hours at the gym, but she knew that her long legs were strong. Her rear was tight—for the most part.

Yet, standing in the middle of the room, naked except for a pair of underwear—with a crotch that was wet from her orgasm—left Bridgette shifting her weight from one bare foot to the other.

"God, you're beautiful," said Luke. "I could look at you all day."

As he watched her, she studied Luke in return. His shoulders were broad. The beginning of a beard covered his cheeks and chin. The fly of his jeans was stretched tight over his erection. She dropped her gaze.

"Look at me," he said again. She lifted her eyes. "Are you uncomfortable being watched?"

Bridgette flipped a lock of hair over her shoulder. "No."

Luke gave a small smile. "Are you lying?"

She shrugged. "I'm not sure."

"I've thought about you over the years," he said. "My fantasies always started out the same. You are standing about where you are now, wearing nothing but your panties."

Running a finger from her throat, between her breasts, she asked, "What else do I do when you think about me?"

"Touch yourself," he said.

Bridgette cupped her own breast, feeling the weight in the palm of her hand. She stroked her thumb over her nipple. In the two years since being a widow, Bridgette had touched herself more than once, yet that was always the most private of moments. What was she willing to do with Luke watching?

Then again, didn't she want to be a fantasy made into reality?

"Like this?" she asked.

"Like that," he said.

She moved her hand lower, skimming her palm over her abdomen and sliding a finger under the fabric of her panties. Her sex was swollen, and the slightest touch sent a surge through her body. She rubbed, unable to control the sensation that built and grew. Closing her eyes, she moaned.

"Look at me," he said, his voice not much more than a whisper.

Bridgette opened her eyes and met Luke's gaze.

"Come here," he said, gesturing to the sofa.

She walked to the edge of the couch.

"Sit," he said. "And spread your thighs."

She did his bidding, light-headed with lust and the game they were playing. Luke knelt on the floor, between her legs, and stroked Bridgette's thighs. His touch was torture—she wanted more of him, needed more.

She fondled her breasts, flicking a thumb over each nipple.

"Don't look away," he said. His breath warmed her core. "I always want you watching."

"Always," she whispered back, as he pulled aside her panties and placed his mouth on her.

Bridgette squirmed beneath Luke's mouth. She wanted to close her eyes and just feel the rush of sensations. But she kept her gaze trained on his eyes as he worked his tongue over her sex and used his fingers inside of her.

In that moment, she left her body, unable to distinguish between her physical self and emotions. She rose higher and higher, leaving the apartment and Braxville and the whole state of Kansas behind. Still, Luke was always there—always watching. His blue eyes became her North Star as she exploded, shattering into a thousand pieces.

Gulping deep breaths, she re-formed into something—someone—brand-new. As if being loved by Luke Walker had rearranged her somehow. She had little time to wonder how. He stood, his gaze never wavering from hers and stripped out of his shirt. Next came his pants—his sex was hard. He rolled a condom down his length and positioned himself over Bridgette.

She tilted her hips, and he entered her slowly. She gasped with pleasure as he withdrew with the same deliberate movements, until just his tip remained inside. Bridgette gripped his ass, urging him to go deeper, harder, faster. She looked down to the point where they joined. Him, inside of her.

They were separate but fitted together perfectly.

"Look at me," he said.

Bridgette was transfixed with the sexes joined and she dragged her eyes away. “Why?”

Luke drove into her hard. “I never want you to think of anyone other than me when we’re together,” he said, slowing his strokes. “For years, I’ve wondered about you. If you’re happy or sad. If you’ve seen the latest movie—and what you thought about it.”

Bridgett reached up and stroked his face.

“Tonight is about more than making fantasies become real. Tonight is about claiming you as mine even if it’s just for a few hours.”

Luke’s breathing increased. His strokes became harder and faster. Bridgette didn’t know that it was possible, but she felt another climax building, a storm gathering in her belly. She cried out with her passion a moment before Luke threw back his head and growled.

For a moment, they stayed on the edge of the sofa, covered in sweat and panting. As Bridgette’s pulse slowed, she moved out from under Luke. “That was amazing,” she said.

“I’ve said this before, but I’ll say it again,” said Luke. “I’m glad you’re back home.” He stood. “I gotta take care of the condom. Stay where you are.”

Bridgette took advantage of the moment alone and redressed in her panties and Luke’s flannel shirt. She stretched out on the sofa. For the first time, she noticed that the apartment was chilly. A blanket was draped over the back of the couch and she pulled it over her shoulders and legs.

For a moment, she stared at nothing.

Hadn’t she vowed not to get involved in life in Braxville? Wasn't she just back for a few weeks to do her job? Her family's involvement in the cancer cases was a problem she hadn't anticipated.

And what about Luke?

And as sleep came to claim Bridgette, even she had to admit that Luke Walker would be an easy man to fall in love with for a second time.

Chapter 17

Bridgette woke, warm and with a feeling of being safe, cherished and loved. For years it was how she began each day—waking in the arms of her husband, Henry. For a moment that reality was as thin as a thread, and she felt as if her husband were still alive. Then the thread snapped, and she lost him all over again. A boulder of grief pressed down on her chest and her eyes burned, filling with tears.

Tears leaked down the side of her face, wetting her hair. Bridgette knew that her first thought upon waking had been right—she was safe and, well, at least cherished. She had fallen asleep on Luke Walker's sofa, and he had joined her. In fact, he slept beside her now, with his arm over her waist.

He was warm and solid. His light snores relaxed away all her tension.

Yet, an ache remained in her chest—the exact spot that hurt every time Henry came to mind. But this time, the pain was bearable. As if maybe—just maybe—the worst of her grief was in the past.

And if that were the case, did she dare to hope for a future?

Luke stirred and drew a deep breath.

"Good morning," he said, placing a kiss on her shoulder.

Bridgette snuggled deeper into his embrace. "Good morning," she said, memories of their lovemaking surrounding her like a fog.

"You looked so peaceful last night, I decided to join you out here."

"I don't mind," she said. "I miss waking up next to someone." She turned to face him and placed her hand on his cheek. "This was nice."

"So, I was thinking that we should spend today here," he said.

"On the sofa?" she asked, teasing.

"If you want…" he began. "Or we can move to the bedroom. Or the shower."

For the span of a heartbeat, she thought about ignoring her job and her duty. She couldn't. Stifling a curse, she sat up. "I can't."

"Can't what?"

"I can't just spend the day with you," she said, rising from the sofa. Her clothes lay across the floor. Stepping into her pants, she continued, "I need to talk to my father about how Colton Construction is the cluster's point of origin." Bridgette paused. "I should probably call Elise Willis, as well."

"The mayor?" Luke sat up. The blanket fell to his lap, revealing his chiseled chest. Bridgette's mouth went dry and she looked away, searching for her socks.

"Why do you want to talk to the mayor?" Luke asked.

"Colton Construction is one of Braxville's major employers. Aside from the economic impact on the town, we very well could have a health crisis."

Luke scratched his chin. "I hadn't thought about the economic impact." He shook his head. "It's hard to imagine folks wanting to visit Braxville if they're going to be exposed to toxins."

"Then you aren't going to like my second concern any more," she said. "All the men who got sick worked at the mall renovation. There's evidence that the carcinogens might be there instead of with the construction company. Elise and I need to discuss if it can safely remain open."

"Shut down the mall before the Boo-fest?" asked Luke. His voice rose an octave. "How is that supposed to make the town look?"

"Responsible," Bridgette snapped. Fully dressed, she grabbed her bag from the coffee table and found her phone. "I'm going to send Elise a text and see when she's available."

After pulling up Elise's contact, Bridgette sent a short message.

I know it's early, Bridgette typed. But we need to meet—today if possible. Important.

Elise replied immediately. I heard you were back in town. Is there something wrong with Neil?

More than being the mayor of Braxville, Elise was also the ex-wife of Bridgette's brother. Bridgette should have anticipated the question. She replied with two words. Work related.

The reply came in seconds. My office in an hour?

It gave Bridgette plenty of time to get ready and collect her data. See you then.

"What'd she say?" asked Luke. Clad only in his boxer shorts, he rose from the sofa.

"I'm meeting her at City Hall in an hour."

"Correction. We're meeting her," said Luke.

"I understand that you're concerned since your father's now part of the cancer cluster. I can't allow family members to be part of the investigation."

"If that's what you think," he said, "then you don't understand at all." Before she could comment, Luke continued. "Julia is still out there, somewhere. Because of me—and our involvement—you're a target for her anger." He paused. "I have no idea what she might do next. Either way, it's my job to keep you safe. Until she's found and getting the help she needs, I'm your new shadow."

In less than an hour, Bridgette was headed to City Hall. As promised, Luke Walker came with her. As always, he wore a flannel shirt and a pair of jeans. It was perfect for the crisp fall weather, and Bridgette had selected an aqua-colored sweater, jeans and boots.

It was Sunday, which in Braxville, meant that none of the businesses were open except the coffee shop. Occasionally, a car drove past. Otherwise, the downtown area was empty and silent.

"I'd forgotten how nice the slower pace of a small town can be," said Bridgette. "In Wichita, there's always busyness and noise. You have to drive anywhere you want to go." She drew in a breath of cool air. "Like I said, this is nice."

Luke hummed an agreement and said nothing more.

She wondered what had him preoccupied, but she had concerns of her own.

A single metal door bisected the back wall of City Hall. Bridgette used her keycard to open the automatic lock. The door clicked and she pushed on the handle.

Without comment, they rode the elevator to the third—and top—floor. The mayor's suite took up a quarter of the story. Elise's personal office overlooked the town park. There was a large wooden desk, along with a bookshelf in the corner. There was also a wine-colored velvet sofa and a matching set of chairs.

"It's good to see you," said Elise, giving Bridgette a quick hug. Elise wore jeans and a button-down blouse. Her dark blonde hair had been pulled into a low ponytail. The mayor looked like she always did—smart, competent, and ready to work for the betterment of the community. "And you, too, Luke." He got a hug, as well. "I have to admit, I was surprised to see your text. You said it's important and work related."

"I recognize this," said Bridgette, running her hand over the sofa's arm.

"You should," said Elise. "Your mother gave me all of this furniture when she redecorated a few years ago." She paused. "Now, have a seat and tell me why you're here."

Bridgette dropped onto the sofa and Luke took a seat in one of the chairs. Elise leaned her hip on the corner of her desk and faced them both. "I'm actually here because of my parents," Bridgette began.

Drawing her brows together, Elise said, "I thought this was business related."

"It is," said Bridgette. "The Kansas State Department of Health has assigned me to investigate a cancer cluster in Braxville."

"I've been briefed."

"Then you know that I'm in charge of the investigation."

Elise nodded. "Have you learned anything?"

"Unfortunately, I have." For a beat, she was at a loss for what to say. "Every one of the cancer victims worked for Colton Construction."

Elise sucked in a breath and leaned back. "Are you sure?"

Bridgette had a file with copies of all her paperwork. "I'm positive," she said, holding out the folder to Elise.

For several minutes, the mayor flipped through the pages without comment. Closing the file, she shook her head. "What do you do next?"

"I have no choice. Colton Construction needs to be closed down," she said, her chest tightening with each word. “We should consider closing down the mall, as well.”

“It will devastate the local businesses if people are worried that they might get sick by going downtown,” said Luke. It was the first opinion he’d offered since they’d arrived.

“They should be worried,” said Bridgette.

“As far as I’m concerned,” said Elise, “public safety is my top concern.”

“If there is something in the mall that’s making people sick,” Luke began, “why are there only a dozen cases of cancer?”

“What do you mean?” asked Elise. “I thought we’d be happy with just a few cases and not a town epidemic.”

“I know what he’s getting at,” said Bridgette. “Hundreds of people go through the mall each day. Thousands in a week. People work there, spending hours of their day. If that’s the case, why would only twelve of them get sick over a span of two decades?”

“Exactly,” said Luke.

“For now,” said Bridgette, a headache forming behind her eyes, “we’ll test air and water quality in the mall. Until we have results, it can stay open. But if there are issues, I have the authority to close down the facility and I’ll use it. No questions asked. Agreed?”

Luke nodded. “Agreed.”

Elise asked, “What are you going to do about Colton Construction?”

“There’s a strong connection to the cancer cases. Until I know that the office compound is safe, I have to close them down and start testing," said Bridgette. "I'm going to visit my dad as soon as we're done here."

"Shouldn't someone else make that visit?" Elise asked.

"No," said Bridgette. "This is my investigation. This is my demand. I'm not putting that responsibility onto anyone else."

"It's also your family and could cause a real dispute between you and your parents." Elise paused. "And there's another problem I can see."

"Which is?" Bridgette asked, her headache intensifying with each beat of her heart.

"If Colton Construction is absolved of culpability in the end, the investigation could look like a sham because you are in charge."

Jaw tight, Bridgette said, "I'm a professional. I can handle it."

"Like you said, it's your decision." Holding out the file Bridgette had brought, she continued, "You'll keep me apprised of any findings?"

Rising to her feet, Bridgette took the folder. "I will, and thanks for meeting with me, Elise. It's good to see you."

"You, too." Elise opened her mouth, seeming to consider what to say next. With a shake of her head, the mayor snapped her jaw shut.

"What did you want to say?" asked Bridgette.

Elise said, "It's nothing."

"It's obviously something. We need to be able to communicate to make it through this investigation. Please, ask me anything."

Elise folded her arms. "How's Neil? I haven't heard from him in a while and, well, I was just wondering."

"I saw him on Friday," said Bridgette. "He was in good spirits. Should I let him know that you asked about him?"

Elise chewed on her bottom lip. "No," she said after a beat. "I'm happy he's doing well."

The conversation wrapped up quickly. Luke and Bridgette left City Hall, and within minutes they were walking down Main Street. "I hate to impose," said Bridgette. "I need a ride to my dad's office. My car was towed yesterday and won't be ready until tomorrow."

"I meant what I said earlier. Until the police find Julia, I'm your shadow." Luke shoved his hand into the pockets of his jeans as he walked. "Why go to your dad's office? It's Sunday morning. Won't he be at home?"

Bridgette shook her head. "Ever since I can remember, Dad's gone to work on Sunday mornings. He says he gets more done if the office is empty."

Luke nodded and they continued to walk. "Are you okay with all of this?" he asked.

Bridgette didn't need him to explain what *all of this* meant. She knew. Moreover, she'd been asking herself the same question.

Could she really be an impartial investigator?

Running Colton Construction was more than her father's job. It was her family's legacy. In a way, the company defined who Bridgette was or, at least, who she had been.

They were at Luke's truck and he unlocked the passenger door before pulling it open. "I'm not sure I'm okay with anything right now," Bridgette said, her tone more resolute than her heart. "But I do know that I have a job to do—and I intend to do it."

Driving on fumes, Julia had left her house in the middle of the night and parked at the back of an abandoned warehouse more than a mile outside of town. From there, she began to walk, terror dogging each step.

Julia was terrified that she'd killed her own mother. Terrified that every passing minute brought her closer to being arrested by the police. Terrified that she'd spend the rest of her life locked up—either in jail or a hospital.

After more than an hour of walking, she realized that her feet had taken her someplace safe. Colton Construction.

Julia had a key to an annex building where the mail was sorted and office supplies were kept. There was a sofa in the room, a coffeemaker and, most important, heat. Despite her constant movement, her hands had turned white with cold and her face was numb.

It was on that same sofa and in that same room that Julia jerked awake. For a moment, she sat up, blinking. Morning sun streamed through the slats of metal blinds. A cup of coffee sat on the floor, a film of creamer floating atop the mud-brown liquid.

Casting a weary gaze around the room, Julia wondered what had woken her suddenly. She heard the low rumble of an engine. Someone had come. But who? Was it the police? Tiptoeing to the window, she pulled aside the blinds and peered into the parking lot.

Dazed, she stumbled back.

Bridgette and Luke, here?

How had they found her?

Sure, there were security cameras on the property. It's just that Julia thought she had avoided them all.

Scanning the room, her heart hammered against her chest—a wild animal trying to break free. There was no way to fight, no way to escape, nothing for her to do beyond give up.

Yet, giving up was something that Julia refused to do.

Fitz Colton had been true to his habits. Aside from Luke's truck, there was only one other vehicle in the parking lot of Colton Construction—the gleaming, white pickup belonging to her father.

"Looks like he's here," said Luke.

Dry-eyed, Bridgette stared out of the window and nodded. "There are two things I value the most," she said. Looking over her shoulder, her gaze met Luke's. "My family and my professionalism. I just never imagined having to choose one over the other."

Luke put the gearshift into Park and turned off the ignition. "You could still have someone else speak to your father. Elise? Somebody from the Kansas Department of Health?"

"I can't shirk my responsibilities," she said. "Shutting down Colton Construction for testing will make my father mad." She paused, knowing that her projection wasn't quite right. She corrected herself, "He'll be humiliated. It's better if the news comes from me."

Luke removed the key. "You know your dad. You may very well be right."

"Besides, he'll want to know what's made everyone sick."

Luke nodded. "You could be right about that, too." Yet, his tone told Bridgette that he thought she was definitely wrong. After a beat, he added, "If you'd rather that I stay in the truck and wait, I can."

"No," she said, maybe a bit too quickly. "I'd like it if you came with me."

Luke nodded. "Are you ready?"

"No," she said. "But let's go."

Bridgette and Luke crossed the parking lot. The main entrance was closed and locked, but as Bridgette and Luke approached, her father opened the door. He was dressed in a dark blue golf shirt, with the Colton Construction logo embroidered on the chest and a pair of jeans.

"Morning," he said, pausing on the threshold. "I saw you on the security camera as you drove up. It's a pleasant surprise to have you drop by and see me."

"Daddy," said Bridgette, her voice small. She held the folder out to her father and continued. "We need to talk."

Her father stepped forward. The door closed and the lock clicked. Taking the file, he drew his brows together and flipped through the pages. "Where'd you get these documents?" he asked, his tone hard.

"Mom had an old box with disks. She gave them to me."

He held out the folder. "It's sad that so many folks in town have gotten ill."

"Daddy, it's not just people in town. It's people who worked for you. Colton Construction is the common thread between the men and their illness." She drew in a shaking breath. "They all worked at the mall renovation, too."

He held the file out farther, implying that if she took the folder all of this would simply go away. Bridgette forced her hands to stay at her sides.

With a shake of his head, her father sighed. "Like I said, it's sad."

Bridgette's pulse raced until it echoed in her ears. "More testing has to be done," she said. "For now, the mall will stay open. I've already talked to Elise."

"Elise Willis?" her father spit. "You talked to her? Really? Why?"

"She's the mayor, and it's her job to protect the public's safety." Another breath. "Colton Construction has to be closed down for testing."

"Closed down? To hell with that plan. Elise hates our family, you know. Your brother Neil, most of all. She'd do anything to get under his skin—including this." He shook the file like an accusatory finger.

"It's not Elise's decision." After folding her arms across her chest, Bridgette met her father's glare. "It's mine."

Her father let out a bark of a laugh. "You had me going for a minute. All this paperwork looks legitimate."

"It's no joke, Daddy. There's something that's making people sick—really sick. It's my job to find out what's wrong and fix it. Until then, this property isn't safe."

"Your job?" Her father's face grew red. A vein appeared on his forehead and began to throb. "What is your job when compared to your family?"

"You need to know what's happening to your employees," Bridgette began. "These folks are your responsibility."

"Don't tell me what I need, missy." Rivulets of sweat ran down her father's face. "I'm your father, dammit. I provided you with that fancy college degree so you could, what? Turn around and use it on me the first chance you get?"

"Mr. Colton," said Luke. "I don't think that Bridgette is being disloyal. What we all want is to find the truth."

With a grimace, he said, "I just want every damn one of you to stop telling me what I want and if you try to close down my business, I'll sue."

"Daddy," said Bridgette. "Be reasonable. We just need to run some tests."

Whatever else she planned to say was forgotten. Her father gripped his shoulder and fell to his knees before toppling, face-first, onto the ground.

Chapter 18

"Daddy!" Bridgette dove for her father.

Luke was right behind her. "Can you hear me, Mr. Colton."

The older man's complexion was red. Sweat streamed down his face, dampening his shirt. "I'm fine," he said, struggling to sit up. "I just got light-headed."

Luke knelt at Fitz's side and pushed his shoulder back down. "Don't try to get up. I'm concerned you're having a heart attack," he said. "Do you take any medications for chest pain?"

With a shake of his head, Mr. Colton said, "No."

To Bridgette, Luke said, "In the glove box of my truck, there's a first-aid kit with aspirin inside. Go and get it."

She returned a moment later, first-aid kit in hand. Luke had already dialed 9-1-1. As she found the foil packet of aspirin, the ambulance was dispatched to their location.

"Here, Daddy," Bridgette said, handing her father two white pills. "You're supposed to chew and swallow these, okay."

Fitz Colton popped the medication in his mouth and began to chew. "They taste like garbage."

"Hopefully, they'll protect your heart," said Luke.

The color in the older man's face had turned from bright red to chalky white. In the distance, the ambulance's siren could be heard.

"Hear that, Daddy? Help's on the way."

Fitz Colton reached for his daughter's hand. "Call your mother and tell her what happened. Can you do that for me?"

"Of course," said Bridgette.

The ambulance sped into the parking lot and stopped next to the front doors. An EMT with a medical kit jumped from the passenger seat. The driver rushed from the front of the vehicle and pulled a stretcher from the ambulance's rear.

"Excuse us," said one of the EMTs, shouldering Bridgette aside.

As the paramedics began to work on Fitz, Bridgette moved to the edge of the sidewalk. Luke followed.

Rubbing her brow, Bridgette said, "I can't believe that I gave my father a heart attack. How can I live with myself if anything happens to him?"

"Hey," said Luke, resting his hands on her shoulders. "You didn't cause anything to happen."

"How can you say that?" She shrugged, trying to

rid herself of his touch. Luke tightened his grip. She continued, "You saw how upset he got when I told him it was my decision to close down Colton Construction for testing."

"If your father had had a heart attack, it was bound to happen. If we hadn't been here, there's no telling how things would have turned out."

"I need to call my mother," she said.

"You don't believe me, do you."

"I don't know what to believe," Bridgette said.

Luke let his hands slip down her arms. "Fair enough."

He stepped aside, giving Bridgette a private moment to speak to her mother. As she ended the call, one of the EMTs approached. "We're taking your father to the hospital for an evaluation."

"We'll be right behind you," said Luke.

They jogged to the truck as the ambulance's lights began to strobe. Bridgette slipped into the passenger seat. "Thank you for taking me to the hospital," she said.

"You don't need to thank me, you know that."

"It seems that I'm turning out to be more trouble than I'm worth."

Putting the gearshift into Drive, Luke maneuvered the truck out of the parking lot and followed the ambulance. "You aren't any trouble at all," he said, knowing that he was dangerously close to losing his heart to her—a woman from his past who didn't want to be a part of his future.

Bridgette could not recall a worse day since her husband, Henry, had died in a car crash. In fact, it was all too familiar. The quiet corridors of the hospital. Worry, a hard kernel, took root in the pit of her stomach. The stench of antiseptic and stale coffee. The hum of fluorescent lights overhead that reflected off tile floors.

She sat in the waiting room, flanked by her mother and Yvette. Everyone had come to the hospital—all three of her brothers, Gwen Harrison, Jordana and Clint, Yvette, Shep. Through it all, Luke stayed. Hour stacked upon hour until she was positive that time would tumble to the ground.

By midafternoon, Dr. Jamapal, a woman not much older than Bridgette with coal-black hair and large, dark eyes, entered the waiting room.

"Mrs. Colton," she said, addressing Lilly.

Bridgette's mother stood. "What happened? How is Fitz."

"Your husband had a blockage in an artery leading to his heart. This broke loose this morning, causing a myocardial infarction. In other words, your husband lost blood flow to his heart and had a heart attack."

"How is he, Doc?" Ty asked.

"At the moment, he's resting."

"What's his prognosis?" Jordana asked.

"He has other blockages that need to be surgically removed. Then, given time to rest and the right rehabilitation, your father can live many more years." She continued, "He was lucky today. If he'd been alone or not have had aspirin administered so quickly, we would be having a very different conversation."

"I'm glad that everything has turned out in the end," said Brooks.

"This isn't the end," said Dr. Jamapal. "But it's not a bad outcome for now. You all can visit your father. The room is small so you might want to take turns. Remember, it's important that he remain calm."

"Thanks, Doc," said Ty. And then the doctor was gone. When the family was alone, Ty said, "There's a lot we have to be thankful for—especially that Bridgette and Luke were with Dad when it happened."

"Yeah, thanks," said Neil. "How'd you even think to give him aspirin?"

"It wasn't me," she said, shaking her head. "It was Luke."

"Because I own a small business," said Luke, "I'm always vigilant about medical emergencies and how important those first few seconds can be."

"It seems like we all owe you our thanks," said Brooks. Then he asked, "Do you two want to go and see Dad first?"

Bridgette shook her head. Her throat was tight, making it hard to breathe and harder still to speak. "You guys go ahead with Mom," she said.

Lilly placed her hand on Luke's shoulder. "Thank you." Then she was gone, leaving Luke, Bridgette and her sisters.

"Are you going to tell me what's going on or not?" Yvette asked. "You haven't said more than two words since we got here, Bridgette."

Her eyes burned. She dropped her gaze to the floor and said, "I should probably go. Luke's been carting me around all day, and he doesn't have this time to waste."

"That's a lame excuse," said Yvette. "And you know it. Spill."

"Dad and I had an argument," said Bridgette. "I'm the reason he had a heart attack."

"You aren't the reason," said Jordana. "You heard what the doctor said. If Dad hadn't gotten immediate care, things would have been worse. It's basically a miracle that you were visiting him when you were."

Bridgette was sick of secrets and always skirting unpleasant truths. "You don't get it," she snapped. "I wasn't just visiting Dad. I was at his office for work." She paused, drew in a breath and met her sister's gaze. "There's a strong link between Colton Construction and the cancer cluster that I'm investigating. The company needs to be closed—at least temporarily—while the state does some testing."

Yvette went white and stumbled backward, as if struck. "And that's when he had the heart attack?"

Bridgette echoed her sister's words, "And that's when he had the heart attack." She dropped her gaze to the floor once more. "So, you can't say that I'm not responsible because, obviously, I am. It was stupid of me to think that I could be the one to deliver such devastating news."

"That's one problem about being a Colton," said Yvette. "Colton Construction is such a big part of life in town that we never really escape it. You know how they found two bodies in the wall of that old warehouse?"

"Of course," said Luke. "It's been all over the news."

"There are people in the police force who don't think

I can be unbiased. They want me to recuse myself from the case."

"You can't be serious," said Bridgette. Anger flowed through her veins. "I'd like to talk to anyone who suggests you aren't completely professional."

"I appreciate your support," said Yvette. "But what I'm saying is that in Braxville, you're a Colton first."

"I know," said Bridgette. For a moment, it felt as if the walls of the small waiting room were moving closer, inch by inch. "I have to get out of here before Mom and the guys come back."

"I understand," said Jordana. "I'll explain to Mom later. And you," she said to Luke. "Take care of her."

"I will."

Bridgette was already gone and striding down the long corridor.

Jogging to catch up, Luke gripped Bridgette's elbow. "Where are you going without me?" he asked.

"I just had to get away."

"I know all of that was hard," he said. "Especially since you are so determined to find out about the connection between the construction company and the cancer cases."

Bridgette nodded as she walked even though she wasn't sure if Luke was right. Bridgette had learned that some things were more important than discovering the truth.

It was her family.

Over the next week, Bridgette developed a routine. In the morning, she went to work. She and Luke spent an hour at lunch taking Pocco, the shelter dog, for a walk. She had dinner with Luke while they worked on the final plans for the Braxville Boo-fest. Since Julia was still at large, she stayed in Luke's apartment.

Bridgette had become more than a guest. She and Luke now shared the master bedroom.

For her, the week had been perfect. There were only two minor—okay, make that major—issues. First, Bridgette had yet to speak to her father. He'd had surgery and was still hospitalized. She had not stopped by to see him, nor had he asked to speak to her. His silence was death by a thousand cuts.

And that brought about her second problem.

Megan Parker's husband had been diagnosed with esophageal cancer. The news had made the rounds in Braxville. Chuck, Megan's husband, was also an employee of Colton Construction.

Bridgette continued to hope that her father's business wasn't involved. The evidence said otherwise. She knew that her job was not worth her relationship with her father. There were other competent people who could take over the investigation. Moreover, as imperfect as Fitz Colton was, he was also her dad.

She woke on Saturday morning, Luke's arm draped across her chest. Her limbs were still loose from the previous night's lovemaking, but her chest was filled with a steely resolve. She didn't care that it was the weekend. Today was the day.

After the parade, she'd call her boss at home and recuse herself from the cancer cluster—the consequences to her career be damned.

Luke stirred, stretched. The covers fell down to his waist, revealing the hard muscles of his stomach and chest. He opened one eye and smiled. "Good morning," he said.

Bridgette couldn't help but smile in return. She stroked his cheek. The short hairs of his day-old beard tickled her palm. "What's got you so happy?"

"I love waking up next to you," he said. "And today is the Braxville Boo-fest. Aside from bringing lots of folks to town, after today I'll be done as the chairman of the festival."

"You think they'll let you go?" Playfully she snapped her fingers. "Just like that? Trust me, Luke. You are a natural-born leader. Honest. Charismatic. Organized. Before long you'll be president of the downtown business association or, worse, mayor."

"I don't want Elise's job, especially with everything that's going on in town with the cancer cluster." He sat up and ran his hands over his scalp, leaving his hair standing on end. "By the way, how's that going. You haven't mentioned anything in the last few days."

"I've made a decision," Bridgette said, rising from bed.

"Oh, yeah? What's that?"

Slipping into a pair of jeans as she spoke, Bridgette said, "I've decided to recuse myself from the case."

"You what?" Luke asked, an edge to his voice.

She slipped a black turtleneck sweater over her head, feeling the heat of irritation rise in her chest. Who was he to take a tone with her? "This case is connected to my family's business. I wanted to think that I could be impartial, but honestly I can't. Every bit of information I uncover leaves me wondering how it affects my father's health. If I'm distracted, I can't be successful."

"So, that's it?" Luke asked, throwing off the covers and getting to his feet. "You're quitting?"

Anger rolled off him in waves, like a hot wind swirling over sand dunes. Bridgette stepped back. "Quitting?" she echoed. "No, of course not. I'm recusing myself from the case."

"Which is a fancy word for quitting."

"What in the hell is your problem?" she asked.

"Cancer ruined my dad's life. You promised me that you'd figure out what happened."

Bridgette searched the floor for her shoes. Where in the hell had they gone? "So, your dad is the only one whose health gets to matter?"

Her argument dampened some of the flames in his fury. "Of course not. That's not what I said—or at least, that's not what I meant."

Pressing her fingertips to her own chest, she continued, "My father had a heart attack. He's in the hospital right now. It's all because of my involvement in the case and the fact that I had to close down his business. Not to mention those cold homicide cases." She waited a beat and then another. "I've lost a child, a husband. I'm not burying my father."

"What upsets me is that you promised to find out what caused everyone to get sick. You said that this was your top priority. You swore to me that you would see this thing through—no matter what. And now, just because things are a little rough, you're done?"

"You're putting words in my mouth."

"But not the sentiment."

There, her shoes were tucked into the corner behind the open bedroom door. She grabbed both boots and sat on the bed's edge. Working her foot into her shoe, she continued, "Besides, it's not as if the case is going to go away. The Department of Health will assign someone else to lead the local team."

"It just won't be you," said Luke, his tone more weary than combative.

Shaking her head, she said, "It won't be."

"Who then?"

She lifted one shoulder and let it drop. "I have no idea, but I'm going to go now. I think we need some time apart, don't you?"

"No," said Luke. "I think we can disagree and still get along."

"I just need a few minutes alone, then," she said. "We have a busy day ahead of us and have to work together to make the parade successful. That won't happen if we're quarreling."

Luke nodded. "Understood."

"I'm going to take Pocco for a walk, first. Then I'll get ready across the hall. I'll meet you at the coffee shop and get ready for the TV interview." She glanced at her phone for the time—6:45 a.m. "At eight o'clock."

Blankets were strewn on the floor. While tossing them back onto the bed, Luke nodded. "See you then."

Without another word, Bridgette left the building. It was the first time in days that she had truly been alone. After years of widowhood, she'd gotten used to her own company. Had being around people so much set her on edge?

Or was the fight with Luke more? Did they really see the world differently? If so, what did that mean for their future? Certainly, she'd be ordered back to Wichita after her recusal. Maybe that wasn't a bad thing.

Maybe it was time to return Luke Walker to her past. And this time, leave him there.

Julia leaned over the steering wheel, straining to see out through the grimy windshield. She had spent the past week in the mail annex of Colton Construction. Closing down the offices had provided her with the perfect place to hide. For days on end, she'd lived on single-brew coffee and stale snacks.

It gave her time to think, to worry, to plan. She'd heard every word spoken between Bridgette and her father. She'd watched all of the state employees conducting tests and had been able to avoid them all.

She knew that Colton Construction had been closed down because of a connection with several cases of cancer. She also knew it was her job to reopen the company.

On Wednesday morning, she woke covered in sweat with her hands trembling. She'd had a dream that left her breathless. It was then that she knew what to do. She took her time going through all the mail that stacked up day after day. She compiled a folder full of documents and bided her time.

It was the morning of the Braxville Boo-fest and Main Street was already busy at 6:45 a.m. She'd parked around the corner. Using the binoculars, she watched the doorway leading to the apartments located above the hardware store.

There were cars parked on both sides of the road. Lights were on in every store, and the windows were decorated with pumpkins, scarecrows, witches and ghosts. Vendors were setting up booths that offered everything from apple cider and doughnuts to custom-created wreaths to antiques to headbands that looked like bat wings and twinkled with purple lights.

None of the activity interested Julia. In fact, the commotion offered the perfect cover. The door opened and Bridgette stepped onto the street. She wore her long hair in a ponytail and shoved her hands into the pockets of a jacket.

Julia expected her to head directly for the coffee shop. Instead, she walked down the street before turning the corner and disappearing from view. Julia started the car and circled the block, not daring to drive down Main Street, where she'd certainly be seen and recognized.

By the time she made her way to the street where Bridgette had been, the other woman was gone. She beat her hand on the steering wheel. "Dammit. Dammit. Dammit all to hell and back," she said, her curses matching the cadence of her heartbeat.

Still, she couldn't have gotten far.

Unless Bridgette had been picked up by someone else. If that were the case, the other woman could be anywhere by now.

Yet, Julia wasn't about to give up—not when she was so close to solving everyone's problems.

On her second circuit through the neighborhood, Julia's luck changed for the better. Bridgette, holding the leash of a black-and-white dog, strode down the street.

"Where did the dog come from?" she asked, knowing what the doctors would say about Julia speaking to people who weren't really there. Then again, the dog wasn't important. What mattered was that she had finally found Bridgette Colton.

Pulling up to the next block, Julia parked and left the car running. She grabbed the folder and stepped from the car.

"Hey, Bridgette," Julia called out. "We need to talk. Do you have a minute?"

Stumbling to a stop, the other woman met Julia's gaze. "You," she said, the single word an accusation.

Julia waved the navy blue folder with the golden Colton Construction logo embossed on the cover like a flag of surrender. Julia said, "I have something you need to see." She was careful to keep her other hand tucked in tight to her leg.

"Do you know how much trouble you've caused?" Bridgette asked. "My car. The apartment's window. Trespassing at my family's lake house."

"I know. I know." Walking toward Bridgette with the folder in her outstretched hand, she continued, "There's something you need to see. It's about Colton Construction and the cancer cases."

Eyes wide, Bridgette blanched. "How do you know about that?"

"I work in the mail room and found some documents you need to see."

The dog began to growl, a low rumble coming from its chest.

"The company has been closed. If you worked there, you'd know that."

"I had an incident with my mom," said Julia, her throat tight. "I've been staying in the trailer because I can't go home. I've seen all the DOH workers taking samples and running tests. I've heard everything you've said to one another. Then, I started looking." She held out the folder farther. "This is what I found."

"What is it?" Bridgette asked, not bothering to step forward.

"I'm not sure," Julia said. "I think it will exonerate your father and Colton Construction of any wrongdoing."

"You do?" Bridgette's face brightened until she almost smiled.

Moving toward Julia, she held out her hand and took the offered folder. The dog began to bark in earnest. "Stop it, Pocco," said Bridgette. "Behave."

Scanning the first few pages of the file, Bridgette drew her brows together. "I don't understand," she began. "None of these documents are connected in any way."

Julia kept her other hand hidden though it trembled. And then, she slipped out of her own body. Like a marionette, her physical self was controlled by an unseen puppeteer. She watched from a distance, breathless with anticipation.

Did the puppet master have the nerve to act?

If Bridgette realized what kind of danger she was in, she didn't show it. Not until she saw the tire iron did her eyes go wide. She screamed—the noise swallowed by the dog's continual barking.

Metal connected with bone and flesh. An arc of blood came off the iron, a comet's tail of gore. Bridgette's eyes rolled into her skull. Falling backward, she hit the ground.

Julia stared at the body and asked herself a single question.

What do I do now?

Chapter 19

Luke Walker held his phone. His grip was so tight he thought the metal and plastic cell might crumple in his hand.

"Have you heard anything yet?" Elise walked across the coffee shop, cup in hand.

The news crew from Wichita had arrived and set up for the interview. Three director's chairs, with the station's logo emblazoned on the seat back, were in a semicircle. Lights shone on the makeshift set, where a blonde anchor read over notes.

Glancing at the screen, he read the long line of messages sent.

I'm here.
At the coffee shop.

Are you on your way?
It's 8:15. Where are you?
Elise just showed up.
The news crew is here. Text me back

And finally, I know we parted ways mad, but don't bail on me now.

There were no replies.

"Nothing," he said.

"It's odd," said Elise. "Bridgette's always seemed so reliable."

With a shake of his head, Luke said, "We argued this morning before she left."

"What about?"

"It doesn't matter now, but I think she might have gone back to Wichita."

"Did she say that?" Elise asked.

Luke opened his mouth, ready to say yes, and then stopped himself. "Not really. She was the one who suggested putting our disagreement aside until after the Boo-fest. Then again," he began, but let his words trail off.

"Then again what?"

He finally gave voice to his fear. "Then again she could have changed her mind."

"It's doubtful. Bridgette is a lot of things—capricious is not on her list." Elise took a sip of coffee and looked out of the window. "I'll be honest, I'm a little worried. Where was she headed after leaving your apartment?"

"She said she was going to the shelter to walk one

of the dogs," he said. "I expected Dr. Faulkner to be here by now, too."

"Maybe there was a problem," suggested Elise.

"I'll call," said Luke, opening his phone's app.

The bell on the coffee shop's door rang, and the old vet—led in by three dogs on leashes—entered. "Sorry I'm late," he said. "I was waiting for Bridgette to come back with Pocco. When she didn't, I figured she'd kept him with her, and they were both here."

"Bridgette's not with you?" Luke asked, his annoyance quickly morphing into alarm.

"No," said the older man. "I haven't seen her since before seven o'clock this morning."

"Excuse me," said the anchor. "Do we have everyone we need for the interview? We go live in three minutes, and you still need to get on your mics."

Luke turned for the door while talking to Elise and the veterinarian over his shoulder. "You both do the interview."

"Where are you going?" Elise called as he pushed open the front door.

"To find Bridgette."

The minute Luke's feet hit the sidewalk he began to sprint. He knew the route she took with the dog. As he ran, he came up with a dozen possible scenarios of what had kept her from her appointment at the coffee shop. Too bad none of them were good.

Three blocks from the shelter, Luke skidded to a halt. Huddling near a fence stood the dog Pocco. The animal's tail was tucked between his legs and he shivered.

"Hey, boy," said Luke, holding out his hand.

Head down, the animal approached. Luke ran his fingers through the dog's short fur. Bridgette was nowhere to be seen.

She'd never abandon her charge while on their walk.

If that was true, where had she gone? Why was she gone?

Luke wrapped his hand around the dog's lead and stepped forward. He stopped, his eye drawn to the seam between street and curb.

A rainbow shimmered atop an oil slick.

Taking a knee, he touched the ground. The oil was still viscous, which meant it wasn't an old stain. His thoughts immediately went to the fresh motor oil they'd found in the woods. He still didn't have any solid evidence that it was Julia who'd been spying that day. Then again, his ex-girlfriend had disappeared soon after, so who else could it be?

And if Julia's car had dripped oil on the street, it meant only one thing—she had Bridgette. Luke had never made a wager, but he'd bet that Bridgette hadn't gone with Julia willingly. The cold hand of dread gripped his heart, his pulse sluggish. He also wasn't the kind to panic, and he pulled the phone from his pocket. He placed a call. It rang twice before being answered by voice mail.

"You've reached Bridgette Colton. I'm not available right now. Leave me a message and I'll get back to you soon."

Cursing, he ended the call.

Phone still in hand, he called Bridgette's sister, Jordana.

Luke had begun to walk again, his hand still wrapped in Pocco's lead.

"It's me, Luke," he said, when voice mail answered. "I think there's something wrong with your sister and I need your help."

He ended that call and placed another, this one to Yvette. It also went to voice mail and he left the same message. Luke placed a call to Bridgette's brother, Brooks Colton. No luck. Then, he called his buddy with the police department, Reese Carpenter.

"Dammit," he said out loud. "Why won't anyone answer their phone?"

The dog looked up and cocked his head. They stood beside Luke's truck, which he had moved away from the downtown festivities to the parking lot of a nearby bank.

For the moment, he'd assume the unthinkable. Julia had kidnapped Bridgette.

Hell, by now, they could be out of state and Bridgette would be gone forever.

No. That wasn't how Julia thought. Everything was a sign. Every place held meaning. Opening the door, he said to the dog, "Come on, boy. Bridgette's missing and we need to find her."

Pocco jumped up and settled into the passenger seat.

Luke turned the key in the ignition and the truck's large engine rumbled to life. He had an idea of where Julia might've gone. He only hoped that they weren't too late.

Bridgette's mouth was dry, and her head pounded. She pried her eyes open and saw nothing but darkness.

She lay on a floor covered in rough carpeting. The scent of motor oil and exhaust hung in the air. Somewhere close was the constant drone of an engine.

"What the hell?" she mumbled through cracked and bleeding lips. Pushing to sitting, Bridgette's head collided with a solid wall, and she slumped onto her stomach again. The aching in her head intensified, and she touched her scalp. Her fingers found a patch that was wet and sticky.

She was bleeding.

What had happened? And, more important, where was she?

Bridgette tried to think and remember. Memories came to her in bursts, like the flash of a camera. The walk. Julia's arrival. The folder full of papers, along with a promise of more information about the cancer cases. Then there was the attack—brutal and brief.

Drawing a lungful of hot air, Bridgette counted to ten and then exhaled. The pain in her head lessened, creating room for her thoughts. First, she knew that she wasn't in a room, but rather the trunk of a car. The rumble of the engine and the jostling of the wheels as they turned were unmistakable.

Which meant that Bridgette had been abducted while unconscious. She knew very little about how to survive a kidnapping other than what she learned in a self-defense class taken in college. Then again, the little bit she remembered might be enough.

The inside of every trunk was equipped with a safety release installed for just such emergencies. Flipping to her back, her hand danced along the lid. She found a plastic handle and pulled.

The latch opened. Blinding and bright, light struck Bridgette in the face. The tires kicked up a rooster tail of dust as the car rumbled down a dirt road. Bridgette didn't waste time with thoughts that might make her lose her nerve. Rising to her knees, she rolled out of the car.

She hit the hard ground at the same moment the car skidded to a stop.

Bridgette's shoulder hurt. Her forearm was scraped and raw. Blood dripped from the side of her hand, and her ankle throbbed with each beat of her heart.

As she struggled to stand, Bridgette cursed. She should have taken a moment to find the car's tire iron. At least then she'd have a weapon, a way to fight back.

"What the hell do you think you're doing?"

She recognized Julia's voice and began to run. Bridgette's ankle collapsed. A tremor of pain ran up her leg as she tumbled to the ground. Julia stalked toward her.

She held the tire iron in her hand, and Bridgette realized she would have searched in vain for it.

"Come back here, you bitch," the other woman said.

Scrabbling backward, Bridgette asked, "Why are you doing this?"

"You know," Julia said.

She was right, Bridgette knew. "Luke," she said.

"You should have just left him alone. I tried to warn you, but you stayed and stayed and stayed." Her face twitched with each word. Foam clung to the corner of her mouth; the tire iron hung in her grip. "He loved me. We were perfect together and you ruined everything."

It was then that Bridgette understood. Julia was more than immature and committed to being bothersome. The other woman was truly obsessed. The life she lived, including her feelings for Luke, had not been rooted in reality. That fact made her dangerous and deadly.

Bridgette knew one thing. She was too injured to fight off another attack. If she wanted to survive, she needed to use her wits. "I'm leaving for Wichita on Monday," she said. "After recusing myself from the Braxville cancer case, I'll be gone. Luke's mad at me. Why don't you just leave me here and go. I won't say anything about what happened."

Julia paused, considering the offer.

Bridgette exhaled a breath she didn't recall holding. Had her argument worked? Had she gotten through to the rational part of Julia's mind?

Then the other woman's face hardened, storm clouds covering a blue sky. "No," she said, her eyes turning black. "It's too late."

"Too late," Bridgette began, as terror gripped Bridgette's throat and her words came out as a squeak. "Too late for what?"

"Too late to let you live."

Grabbing Bridgette by the arm, the other woman pulled her to her feet.

Bridgette's vision exploded in a flash of white. The pain from her head injury made it hard to breathe and harder still to think. Yet, she had to get away from Julia.

Marshaling all her strength in her shoulder, she

swung her arm in a wide arc. Her fist connected with the side of Julia's head. The impact sent the other woman staggering back and her grasp faltered.

Bridgette didn't take in her surroundings and began to run.

A road led through a heavily wooded area. She clambered over a rotted tree trunk. In a flash of memory, she recalled Luke jumping over the very same log. That meant they were in the woods near her family's lake house.

Pain radiated through every part of Bridgette's body. She shoved all her discomfort aside and forced her legs to move faster. Bushes and shrubs on either side of the trail passed as a blur.

Ahead, Julia stepped out from behind a tree. Her dark hair was wild, and tendrils obscured her pale face. Her shoulders were hunched forward. In her hand was the tire iron. Bridgette slowed, spun and began to run the other way.

Sweat streamed down Bridgette's face, stinging her eyes and blurring her vision.

Then a pain exploded in the back of her head. She knew she'd been hit once again while stumbling forward. As she fell, the forest floor disappeared and a bottomless chasm opened. Bridgette continued to fall, surrounded by nothingness.

She tried to scream but could make no sound.

Her eyes were heavy and her limbs were weary, aching all the way to her bones. Sleep called to her with a siren's song.

Yet, if she gave into the desire for rest, she would

never wake again. Forcing her eyes to open, she saw the sky and dappled sunlight streaming through the treetops that towered above. There were hands under her arms. The ground was rough at her back as she rolled over twigs and stones.

She was being dragged. But where was she being taken?

A beam of light caught her in the face. The light seared her pupils and she screwed her eyes shut. She tried to pry her lids open. It didn't work.

Then she was falling again.

This time she didn't care.

The blackness was inviting and seductive. It was the open and waiting arms of a lover. She longed to be lost in the oblivion it offered.

Then for a moment Bridgette went cold. She felt a breeze on her face. She was weightless and out of control.

She landed on her back.

Icy water slapped her in the face. All the air was driven from her lungs. Her mouth filled with cold and slimy debris. She began to cough. Her arms and legs swung out in wild arcs.

It was then that all of Bridgette's faculties returned.

She was at the bottom of a well, the same one she had loved as a child. This time there was no magic to save her. She was trapped. The walls were covered in slick black slime, making climbing out impossible.

Treading water, Bridgette looked up. The sky, a blue disk, was visible at the mouth of the well. The opening was less than a dozen feet away—it might as well have been miles.

Standing in the sunlight and looking down was Luke's ex—Julia. With a smile, the other woman flipped the metal door closed. It hit the well's stone lip with a clang, surrounding Bridgette in darkness.

Important life moments rushed by. Luke's face filled those memories more than once. His was the touch she craved, and his voice was the one she longed to hear. Sure, she'd only been back in Braxville for little more than a week. But she'd known from the beginning that she and Luke were meant for one another.

How could Bridgette have let his love slip away for a second time?

Paddling her feet, she treaded water to stay afloat. Her arms ached and her legs were heavy. She could feel the cold water pulling her down.

Nobody knew where she'd gone—or maybe even suspected that she was missing. It was here, at the bottom of this well, that she was going to die.

Luke pressed his foot on the accelerator as the speedometer climbed to seventy miles per hour. Eighty. Ninety. He completed the half-hour drive to Lake Kanopolis in less than fifteen minutes.

Swerving onto the short drive leading to the Colton fishing cabin, he slammed on the breaks, the grille of his truck inches from the wall. With the engine still running, he leaped from his truck and sprinted to the door. He turned the handle—it didn't budge. Lifting his foot, he made ready to kick in the lock. His phone rang. Standing upright, Luke removed the phone from his jacket and checked the caller's ID.

It was Elise. The reception was lousy, with only a single bar of coverage.

Swiping the call open, he said, "Tell me you have Bridgette with you."

"No, that's why I'm calling. Where are you two?" she said, her words filled with static. "The festival has started, and we need our chairperson."

"You have to take care of this without me," he said. "I'm at the Coltons' cabin."

"Did you just say the Colton lake house?" she asked. "What? Why?"

Luke took only the briefest moment to tell her about finding the shelter dog on the street along with the suspicions that his ex-girlfriend had something to do with Bridgette's disappearance. He ended the story with, "I had a feeling that Julia brought Bridgette out this way, but it doesn't look like anyone has been at the house since we left last week."

"Lake Kanopolis is huge," said Elise. "Bridgette could be anywhere."

Luke searched the expanse of water. A veil of fog hung over the surface, and he couldn't help but wonder what was hidden in the depths. Yet Julia wouldn't have simply taken Bridgette someplace random. That was why the fishing cabin had come to mind. It was a special place for Bridgette and Luke's relationship.

"I'm not leaving until I have a chance to look around," he said. "You'll take care of the Boo-fest for me?"

"Of course, and I'll find Jordana. We'll get the police looking for both Julia and Bridgette in case either one is still in town."

Luke didn't bother thanking the mayor or even ending the call. He turned off the truck's ignition and began to run. Frantic barking jerked him to a stop. He didn't have time to deal with an animal. Then again Pocco might be able to help. Retracing his steps, he opened the passenger door.

Jumping to the ground, the dog began to snuffle.

"Do you have her scent, boy?" he asked, picking up the lead that still trailed from the dog's collar.

Pulling on his leash, the animal forced Luke to run in order to keep pace. By the time they reached the well, Luke's breath came in ragged gasps. The metal door was closed, but the rusty chain had been shattered, and pieces were scattered on the ground.

Pulling free of the leash, Pocco began to whimper and paw at the ground around the well.

Luke raced forward and lifted the heavy metal door.

There, looking up from the gloom, was Bridgette Colton.

Holding tight to the webbed fabric, Luke dangled Pocco's lead into the well. Bending at the waist, he stretched down. Bridgette reached upward, her fingertips grazing the leash.

"You can do it," he said. "Just a little higher."

"I can't," she said, batting at the handle. Her touch sent the leash into a lazy circle.

Dammit. Bridgette was right. She was reaching up as far as she could. If he bent down farther, they'd both end up in the water. He had rope in his truck, but he dared not leave her alone.

It was then that Luke realized he didn't need a rope—only something strong that could make the leash a bit longer.

"Hold on a second," he said. "I know what to do."

Bridgette looked up. Her wide eyes were filled with terror but also hope. "You aren't leaving me here, are you?"

"I'll be right here the whole time. I promise."

Luke straightened and unbuckled his leather belt. He wrapped it through the leash's grip, creating a loop that Bridgette could grab. He lowered the lead and Bridgette took hold of the belt. He began to pull.

Bridgette rose from the water. She pushed her feet into the wall of the well, transferring some of her weight and helping her ascent.

Upward she rose, inch by inch. Stone bit into Luke's middle. White-hot pain filled his shoulder. His legs trembled with fatigue. He ignored the pain and continued to pull.

Bridgette was mere inches from Luke. He reached to her. Her fingers interlocked with his. With all his strength, Luke hauled her out of the well. He toppled back and Bridgette landed on his stomach. She was cold and wet. Her body trembled, not solely from the chill.

"I thought I was going to die," she said, her voice thick with emotion. "How did you find me?"

"I found him," said Luke. After helping Bridgette to sit up, he hooked his thumb toward the dog. Head down and eyes up, the dog approached. Reaching out,

Luke ruffled Pocco's ear. "He was alone on the street. That's when I knew something had happened to you. I saw a fresh oil stain on the ground, just like we saw in the woods. I figured Julia was involved. I had a hunch that she'd come to the lake."

"Thank goodness you listened to your instincts." She drew in a deep breath. "It was Julia. She said she had information about the cancer cluster and how Colton Construction wasn't involved. It was all a ruse. She told me that she worked in the mail annex—had been hiding there while the offices were closed—and had found some paperwork. She even had a Colton Construction folder and everything. I wanted to believe and didn't worry about being careful."

Luke's phone began to ring. He glanced at the screen. "It's your sister," he said, handing over the phone.

"I still can't believe you have coverage all the way out here," Bridgette said, swiping the call open. For a moment, she spoke, giving her sister the details of what had happened. It was hard for Luke to listen. He never should have left Bridgette alone, especially since he knew that Julia was dangerous.

She ended the call just as the sounds of sirens could be heard in the distance. "Yvette said she called the ambulance."

"That must be them," said Luke, helping her to stand. He held her close until the EMTs arrived and Bridgette was moved to the rear of the ambulance, where she was evaluated.

He stepped away and placed a call to Reese Carpenter. Pocco ambled next to Luke and sat as the phone began to ring.

"Luke," he said. "What's up?"

"I have Bridgette with me, but Julia needs to be found before anyone else gets hurt."

"Every police officer in the state is looking for Julia right now."

"Bridgette mentioned that she'd been hiding in the mail room at Colton Construction for the past week. It's a trailer located at the rear of the property."

"I'll check it out now."

"Thanks, man," said Luke. "I appreciate it."

After ending the call, he approached the ambulance. Bridgette sat on a stretcher in the rear cabin with the back door open. "What'd the EMTs say?" he asked.

"I need to be evaluated further at the hospital," she said. "I'll call you once I know anything."

"Are you trying to get rid of me?" he asked.

"Today is the Braxville Boo-fest. You've worked hard to make it successful. Certainly, you want to be there. It's important."

"You are important to me, Bridgette." He paused. "If you want me leave you alone, tell me. Otherwise—I'm going to be with you now and later."

"Luke, I…"

Before she could continue, one of the EMTs approached. "Excuse me, sir," the other man said, slamming the door shut. "We have to take the patient to the hospital."

Lights strobing and siren wailing, the ambulance sped away.

Luke watched as the ambulance rumbled over the woodland track. Were the police on the way, ready to search the woods and the lake for Julia? Or would they come to the well and collect evidence? He assumed so, but for now, it was silent.

Birdsong filtered through the woods. The sun climbed higher, warming the morning and promising that it was going to be a perfect fall day. Luke had confessed that he wanted a future with Bridgette. What would she have said if they hadn't been interrupted?

The dog leaned into his leg, giving a contented sigh. "What do you think, boy?" Luke asked. "Should we go after her?"

Pocco looked up as Luke spoke.

"I agree completely," he said to the dog. "We can't give up now."

Chapter 20

Julia had no place else to go and returned to the mail annex. Her brow was covered in sweat and her pulse resonated in her skull. She sat in the corner, her knees pulled up to her chin, and wondered how long she would feel sick.

Was this a fleeting sensation?

Or would Julia be overwhelmed with guilt for the rest of her days.

She hadn't meant to kill Bridgette and that was a fact.

Yet, there was another fact, one that Julia couldn't avoid. The other woman was most certainly dead by now.

And dead was dead. There were no do-overs.

For the first time in months, the scars on Julia's wrist began to itch.

She scratched, her nails leaving red welts on her skin.

"Julia Jones, this is Detective Reese Carpenter with the Braxville Police. Come out of the trailer with your hands up." The voice boomed through a PA system.

Dammit. She should have left her car at the old warehouse and not driven back to Colton Construction.

"Julia," he said again. "You have to come out or I will come in and get you."

She crawled across the floor, careful to stay below the windows. There, on the shelves, was a box cutter. Still on her knees, she reached up and grabbed the knife.

Julia scuttled back to her corner. She looked at her wrists. The lines were already there. She pressed the knife's tip to her flesh. Harder. Harder. The blade sliced her flesh and her arm began to weep blood.

The door opened with a bang.

Reese Carpenter and Jordana Colton stood on the threshold. Both had their guns drawn.

"Put down the knife, Julia," said Jordana, hand lifted. "You don't want to hurt yourself or anyone else."

"Don't I?" Julia spit. "I hurt my mother. I killed your sister. I'm a bad person." She shoved the knife deeper into her arm. There was a flash of pain, white-hot, and blood began to drip onto the floor, soaking into the dirty carpeting.

"My sister's not dead," said Jordana. "And your mother misses you. She wants you to come home—not die."

"Momma?" Julia asked. Her resolve wavered.

She should have never let her guard down.

Before she realized that he'd moved, Reese Carpenter had Julia's wrist tight in his grip. The flow of blood was now a trickle. She was on her feet, her back pressed to his chest. The knife lay on the ground, surrounded by a puddle of blood.

Bridgette was evaluated by Dr. Jamapal, the same physician who had seen her father only days before. The diagnosis: a mild concussion, scrapes, bruises, a cut to her scalp that needed stitching, and hypothermia from being submerged in the cold water.

Considering everything that she'd endured, Bridgette was lucky to be alive.

"I'm keeping you overnight for observation," said the doctor. "The man who followed the ambulance, Luke Walker, is in the waiting room. Would you like to see him?"

"Sure," said Bridgette, pushing up to sitting.

The doctor left, and a moment later the door opened. It wasn't Luke who entered the room—it was her father. He was still a patient at the hospital and wore a robe over a set of sweats.

"Daddy?"

"Hey, honey, I heard you were here. Can I come in?"

She bit her bottom lip, stanching her tears of love and disappointment. "Of course," she said. "I'm sorry that I haven't stopped by this week. I feel, well, responsible for what happened. More than that, I was worried that you blamed me for your heart attack."

"To be honest, until I heard that you'd been attacked, I did blame you. Then I realized that there's nothing more important than you and my other kids."

"I've decided to recuse myself from the investigation. I tried to be a good scientist and not let anything other than the facts form my opinions. But you and your health are important to me—as is our relationship."

"I'm not asking you to step away from the case because of me."

"You didn't have to ask," she said.

Her father sat on the edge of her bed. Rubbing a hand over his chin, he exhaled. "You know, there's something I should probably tell you about what's happening in town." The door opened. Fitz Colton stopped talking.

Luke stood on the threshold. "Sorry for interrupting," he said. "I thought you were alone."

"I just had to check on my baby girl."

"Well, I'm glad you're both here," he said. "I got a call from Jordana. She and Reese found Julia."

"Really? Where?"

"She was hiding in the mail room of Colton Construction, just like you said."

"Colton Construction?" her father echoed. "What in the world is happening?"

"Julia worked in the mail room, but there's more to the story," said Bridgette. "It sounds like there's a lot for us to discuss."

"Do you need a minute?" Luke asked, hooking his thumb toward the door. "I can give you some privacy."

Bridgette's dad stood. "I'm the one who should be going. I'll call your mother and give her an update. I'm sure she'll be down to visit shortly. I just wanted to see you first."

"Daddy," she said as he reached the door. "What was it that you wanted to tell me?"

He waved her question away. "It'll keep. You get some rest."

Luke moved to Bridgette's side and took her hand in his. "How are you feeling?" he asked.

She answered his question with one of her own. "If you've been here, then where's Pocco?"

"My dad stopped by and picked him up. If I know my dad, he's probably sharing a sandwich with the dog right now."

Bridgette laughed. "He's a good dog. I wish he would find his forever home."

"Funny that you'd say that. I'm pretty sure that someone plans to adopt Pocco."

"Really? Who?"

Luke shrugged. "Me."

"You?"

"We made a pretty good team in finding you." He lifted her hand and placed a kiss on the inside of her wrist. "But you never answered my question. Honestly, how are you?"

"I'm sore. I'm tired. I'm thankful to be alive." Yet, there was more to talk about than her health. "When I was in the well," she began, "I thought there was no way I would ever get out. There were a lot of things for me to regret. The one that came to mind again and again was that I never would be able to see what the future would hold for you and me."

"Future?" he echoed, reaching for her hand.

"I realized something important," she said, unwilling to stop speaking now that she'd begun. "Over the years, I'd lost people I loved—the baby, Henry. I thought that the best way to avoid pain was to live behind an emotional wall. With you, I couldn't hide. I'm happy to be alive because it gives us another chance." She paused, bit her bottom lip. "That is if you'll have me."

"Bridgette, I loved you when we were kids and I've never stopped. All this time, there was something missing in my life. I now know what it is," he said.

"Oh, yeah, what's that?" she asked.

"You."

Luke leaned forward, placing his lips on hers. The kiss was tender, loving and meant to last a lifetime.

* * * * *

Don't miss the next exciting story in
The Coltons of Kansas:

Colton Storm Warning *by Justine Davis*

SPECIAL EXCERPT FROM

HARLEQUIN

ROMANTIC SUSPENSE

The last time he lost a witness, Detective Jack McTavish nearly lost his job. Now protecting Greta Renault, an artist who witnessed a murder, is his top priority. As he's forced to choose between believing her and saving his career, Jack's decision could make the difference between life and death.

Read on for a sneak preview of Guarding His Midnight Witness, *the next book in the Honor Bound series by Anna J. Stewart.*

"Don't! I saw him. He was here." Her mind raced. Her ankles wobbled in the ridiculous shoes Yvette had convinced her to wear. Swearing, she reached down and slipped them off, leaving them on the sidewalk as she sped down the street toward the historic section of the building. He couldn't have gotten very far. He could even be back inside. Maybe he'd gone up instead of down. Maybe… He had to be here somewhere. She spun in circles. She wasn't imagining things. She had seen him. He'd seen her. And there… She froze. Her breath went cold in her chest. She stared across the street to beneath the blinking pedestrian-crossing light.

"Greta." Jack's hands reached out for her.

She tore herself away. Falling, flailing. Horns blared.

HRSEXP0920

Tires screeched. She hit the pavement. Hard. Pain blazed up her arm and across her cheek as the world went into slow motion.

Voices exploded around her, concerned, frantic voices, demanding ones. Angry ones. She felt herself being pulled up, first into a sitting position where she found Jack bending over her, hands pressed on either side of her face as he said her name over and over. "Greta. Come on, Greta. Talk to me. You all right?"

"Yes," she finally managed to say and grabbed hold of his wrists. She blinked up at him, touched by the fear and concern she saw in his eyes even as the expression pushed her further inside herself. "I'm okay. Let me up."

A few more voices echoed around her before Jack hauled her up and led her out of the street and over to where she'd dropped her shoes. He scooped them up, and they claimed a small bench in front of the museum.